RED AND THE
CURSE OF THE UNSPEAKABLE

Lisa, words have sorry.
words have power. Choose them wisely! remember your words when you say you are worthy!

1

Prologue

Long ago, in a peaceful village, a beautiful woman became of marrying age. Unhappy with the choice of husbands in her own tribe, she decided to look outside of her village for a mate.

Men came from miles away and presented themselves for her approval. Most of the men that she declined walked away without a word, but there was one man who was just as vain as the woman. Unbeknownst to her, this man was a powerful sorcerer. When the woman told him he was not worthy of her, he became enraged and cast an Unspeakable Curse on not only her but on her entire tribe.

"Your words, they've cut me like a knife,
So, from this day forward, you will be no man's wife;
Your village, all prisoners of the Unspeakable Curse, a fate for you, I can think of no worse.
Carefully now, for your words you must choose,
or this curse will take hold, and your life... you may lose."

At that very moment, words had become weapons that were best avoided.

In time, the once-beautiful woman grew old and died, unwed, of course, and for generations afterwards, the "Curse of the Unspeakable" lived on.

I would like to dedicate this book to my
father, you are missed every day.

To my husband and son, for making me laugh.
I love you.

To my daughter, for always encouraging me,
I love you.

Thank you, to my family, friends, and everyone who
believed in me.

Most importantly, Maria Lepage;
You are such a great friend;
I would be lost without you.

This book is a complete work of fiction. Any
character(s) name used by the author that may resemble
a real person is strictly coincidental. All names and
situations are from the imagination of the author.

Cover design by Toby Gray
Edited by Cheryl Whittier
Copyright © 2012 Maryellen Worrell

Chapter 1
Red

In a village where no words were spoken, Red was born on a quiet, still day. No clouds cluttered the sky, no birds flew above his village, and no elders gathered at the fire pit to breathe in the Breath of Life. It was customary for the elders to gather, breathe the sacred breath, and announce the name of their newest, silent members.

Usually, when the first child was born to a clan member, there would be a large celebration that lasted for days and days. Elders would dress in their finest animal skins and feathers. The expecting fathers would climb the tallest mountain, climb the tallest tree, cut down the longest branch, and carve a crib from the strongest wood. Village men would hunt for the largest boar to roast for the celebratory meal, while women picked the freshest fruit, which grew on the outskirts of the village.

Then, there would be the honorary bead-making, in which every clan member would wear the beaded necklace with intricate patterns, representing their father. The children would have been set to the task of dyeing the beads; as it kept their hands busy, while the others gathered the special wood for the Fire of Life ceremony.

So much to do when a child was born, but, when you are the seventh son with six older sisters, there is nothing to do. No celebration, no bead necklace presented on the day of his birth, no roasted boar, and no crib made from the strongest tree branch. Certainly, there was no Fire of Life to pronounce the name given, for there was no name left to give. What do you call the thirteenth child born, except for the color of the worn out birthing bed?

With a sigh of relief, Shelu, the now exhausted mother, gently held her newborn baby.

"I name you, Red," she whispered, as she kissed him tenderly. After birthing so many children, her body was now so weakened that it no longer could support her any longer. Using all the last strength she had left inside, Shelu held her newborn close to her, as she sensed the Spirits surrounding them. She held his tiny head against her and sang barely above a whisper. She softly sang to him the tribal blessing. She sang of birds dancing in the morning sun. She sang of the wolf dancing before the harvest moon, but mostly, she sang of a mother's love for her son.

She silently thanked the good spirits who had allowed her this one gift of song, and as she did, she fell asleep, still holding Red in her lifeless arms, and in that following instant, Shelu had taken her last breath.

Chapter 2
The Journey to Manhood

Red grew up in a non-verbal tribe without his mother. He never understood what caused her to die on the day of his birth. Due to the curse, he was unable to ask his burning question. He often wondered what life would have been like, had his mother survived that night. How different would his childhood have been?

While he was still very young, Red's favorite place to be was the school hut, as it was the only place where the children were able to laugh, and play, and speak freely. It was built after the Elders had prayed to the spirits for guidance to help protect the innocence of the children and to give them a safe place to learn. Their answer came in the form of a vision.

They were instructed to stand around the school hut, hold hands, and chant their tribal name in unison until lightning struck the hut. With their united words, they had summoned the needed lightning. Amazingly, rather than cause a fire, it caused the entire school to turn black as night. Once the school hut had blackened, the elders along with the good Spirits, felt a "Spell of Protection", instantly encompass the hut. Since that day, the elders knew that the children's words would be protected inside the school hut, at least until they were considered to be no longer of school age.

Today, Red turned fifteen. In the eyes of the Elders, he was almost a man and would no longer be shielded by the protection of the school hut. Red stepped out of his own hut, dressed in his usual tribal skins, with his short dark hair in its usual disarray. He walked slowly away from his hut and noticed the village elders all gathering in front of him. The elders now circled around Red, and as he stopped, they closed the circle behind him. They began chanting the tribal name over and over again. He just stood still and listened to their sound with his eyes closed and his mouth turned up in a small grin. He knew that this was the clan's "birthday" ritual and it pleased him to be considered a man now, rather than a child.

He had already learned so much from his teacher, an elder named Paw. He wisely taught him well, especially "Words have power, always choose them wisely." On this special day, the elders reminded him once more. From that day forward, Red noticed his words began to make things happen.

Aware of his new ability, Red wanted to explore the power of his voice, even if it was a curse that caused it, and even though he was warned against it. Defiantly, yet cautiously, he had stood far away from his hut, with no one in sight and then Red spoke three little words.

"Make me fly."

Instantly, his feet began to lift off the ground a few inches. Afraid he would fly away, Red stretched out his arms for balance. Nervously, he said "down." His feet and body started back toward the ground. Red was impressed but very wary about what he had done. Even though nothing bad had happened yet, he know the elders were wise and if they warned him about using his words, then surely not heeding their advice, could lead to trouble. Since that day he was very careful when choosing to speak. He now knew, first hand, that this magnificent ability was real and could prove dangerous, as the elders often reminded.

A few days later, not too far from the day that he "tested" the curse, all of the elders surrounded Red again and began chanting the tribal name. Once again, Red knew enough to be still. It was known throughout the clan that when the elders surround you, it is a time to stop and listen. Soon voices were as one as Red's vision became blurry and smoke filled the air. He felt as though he was stepping into another time and place, yet he was sure that he had not moved. Smoke continued to appear and was coming from beneath his feet, from Mother Earth, herself. Red could barely see the figures standing around him. Out of all the blurry figures he saw before him, only one figure stood out from all the others and stepped forward. It was a woman, taller than he, and incredibly beautiful. She was the only one that he could see clearly. As she came closer and closer to him, her eyes fixed upon his, while her dark green eyes met his matching reflecting ones. Suddenly, Red sensed something familiar and comforting. He somehow knew who this wondrous woman was. Amazingly, he was now face to face with... his mother.

Shelu stepped forward, with swirling smoke still rising from the earth, encircling her as if it were going to, once again, conceal her and take her away. Her mouth moved, but Red did not hear a sound. Strangely, when her lips stopped moving, he could then, hear her soft voice.

"Red, my son," she said, in a tender, motherly tone. "It does me good to see you. When last we were together, it was the first day of your life and the last of mine. I rest well knowing that you will be a fine man." She said this, as if she had already seen his entire life from beginning to end, and was merely stating a fact. Again, her lips began to move and just as before, Red heard nothing. Finally, after her lips stopped, he heard her silky voice, once again.

"I have been summoned here by the elders to help you begin your journey. It is up to me, as your mother, to start the task of enlightenment. When you awake, you will no longer be in the Bonk Bonk village.

During this time, you will no longer be my son. You will leave all your family behind, until you can find your way home. When you can find your way back to the elders, then you will be a man. You, my son, will have proven that you belong to the Bonk Bonk tribe. Go forth and fear not. Use your head and choose your words wisely, for they have more power than you know. Keep with you the knowledge that the Spirits will be with you. Awake now my son, and feel the new earth beneath your feet. Your journey begins as this new air becomes your next breath."

Shelu stepped back into the white smoke and disappeared. Just then, Red's vision became clear again. He blinked and was amazed when he looked around.

Red stood in a forest, with trees so tall that he could barely see the tops. The earth that he now stood upon was warm instead of cool. In the Bonk Bonk village, the ground was always cool. He was not sure if it was due to the closeness of the seaside or if it was the red clay earth. Now in this strange land, Red squished his bare toes into the grass, until he made a small hole in the ground. He could not wait to feel the earth that lay beneath the green grass. Like putting on a warm blanket, his feet felt warmer once they were buried underneath the brown dirt.

He kept digging at the hole until it was large enough to stick both feet in. While happily warming his feet, Red heard a sudden and unusual sound that resembled a large grumbling noise. Suddenly, the earth beneath his feet began to shake. Losing his balance, he stumbled to the ground and landed on his back side with his feet in the air. *This new land has spoken to me. I must have made it angry,* Red thought.

Quickly, he righted himself and stood up. He noticed that the smell in the air was different from what it had been just a moment ago. While searching for where the odor was coming from, he could see that off to the far west, was a mountain that had black smoke coming from its peak. As quickly as he could, Red replaced the grass to its rightful place, hoping he would no longer anger the earth. With his head bowed deeply, Red thought, *Forgive my ignorance, Mother Earth.* He hoped he had made amends, but just in case, he took off running towards the east.

He passed hundreds of trees that were so tall that the tops could hardly be seen. As he ran, not only was the ground becoming less warm, but the trees were also looking smaller and smaller. Red wondered if they would soon become low enough, so that he could simply pluck them, like a flower. With the trees low now, he could see that the leaves were brittle and brown.

The day started turning into night. Red ran until he was breathless. He stopped briefly to catch his breath again and then he began to walk. He walked until he could not take another step.

Red found a large boulder he could sit on and rest his exhausted feet. The boulder was half his height but twice as long as him and completely flat on top. Red climbed up the boulder and took in his surroundings.

Since it was dusk, he could still see clearly, with just a hint of dark shadows behind the trees. He knew that he would soon need food, but first, he needed rest. He decided to lie down, and before he knew it, he fell asleep.

Chapter 3
The Little House

In the morning, when Red had awakened, he rubbed his eyes and thought, *time to find breakfast*. Red looked around for something that he could eat. He jumped off the boulder when he heard breakfast calling him. As he looked up in search of the sounds, he saw birds singing their morning song. Red knew where there were birds, there had to be eggs as well. Slowly, he walked around looking up at the trees. These trees looked easy for him to climb and besides, there were plenty of branches and large roots coming from the ground to give him a leg up, if needed.

Red found a bird perched on a tree limb. *Ah there it is*, thought Red. He looked to the right of the bird, and then to her left. Next he noticed that above the bird, was indeed a nest. So he began to climb, scaring the bird away. With the tree being rather easy to climb, he came upon the nest in no time. There, waiting for him, were four small blue, speckled eggs. He scooped them up and ate them, shells and all.

As he began to climb back down the tree, he noticed a little house in the distance. It had a roof made of old dried tree limbs that were dark and weathered, as well as a little stone chimney that did not have any smoke coming from it. Red was the curious type and decided he would go investigate. Maybe someone there could tell him exactly where he was.

Once Red was out of the tree, he began to walk toward the little house. It was a longer walk than he expected because when he was in the tree it did not look so far away. The closer he came to the house, the slower he walked. Keeping close to the trees, he walked softly, to make as little noise as possible. Every step was calculated and planned. He continued forward, all the while watching for movement in the house. His plan was simple. He did not want to be seen until he was at the front door. Caution told him that whoever lived here might not welcome a stranger. He took his time making his way, until finally the door to the little house only stood ten feet to his right.

The little house was set alone in the woods. There were no gardens and no barns for cattle or horses. There were no stacks of fire wood waiting for winter to be burned. There was nothing around but growing trees. Not one thing about this house made him think that anyone was inside it. Rocks made up the foundation, and weathered tree limbs were the walls. Oddly, it also had just one little window. It did not appear to be a house that one would make into a home. It looked too quickly assembled, like the builder was in a rush. *But then, why build a window or foundation?* He supposed he would never know the answers, since it looked deserted, even close up.

Red went to the door, knocking gently at first. When no one answered the door, he knocked louder and harder. Still no one answered. Strangely, Red could not see a door knob, which made him wonder how the door was being kept closed. He thought the force of his knock would cause the door to break. Even though the door looked hastily made, it was strong and did not waver.

Finally, Red decided to speak to the door, "unlock and open." Just then he heard a click come from the other side of the door. A few seconds later, the door creaked open, causing the hairs on Red's arm to stand on end. Nervously, he stepped through the doorway.

Once inside, he noticed the window provided plenty of light to see. There was a table directly in the center of the room. He looked around and noticed a three-legged chair tipped over on its side. The broken chair leg was on the floor between the table and the fireplace that was against the far wall. There were spider webs hanging from the corners of the room and a thick layer of dust covered everything in sight.

On the same wall as the fireplace, there was another door. Red walked over to it, seeing no door knob, he pushed on it. When that did not work, Red again used his words and said, "Unlock and open." As commanded, the door did just that. It swung open, and what lay inside the tiny room surprised him. A large silver-haired dog with long shaggy fur was lying on the floor. If Red was not mistaken, this dog not only had long eyebrows, but he also had an even longer beard and mustache.

The dog lifted his head, stretched out his two front paws, lifted his hind quarters slightly up into the air, and stretched. The dog yawned and said, "Well, it's about time you showed up, my boy."

Standing in shock, Red's mouth hung wide open. Frozen, he did not know what to do. *Did that dog speak,* he thought. When the dog stood up on all four legs, his back was as high as Red's chest, far larger than the average height of a dog.

As the dog passed the door's threshold, the frame began to sparkle and glow. It began to glow even brighter than the door frame. Once completely out of the tiny room, the dog, still glowing brightly, began to transform.

Chapter 4
Alexandros the great ......Dog?

With his mouth open in awe and unable to look away, Red watched the dog glow brighter and brighter. *In all my life I have never seen such a sight,* he thought.

The dog walked to the table and rested its front two paws on it. It began to breathe heavily. He threw his head back in one quick jerk, as if it were going to howl but, instead of howling, the dog's front legs began to shorten and transform into human arms. His rear legs straightened into human legs, and his dog head swelled into a human head with human eyes, ears and nose. Its tail shrunk inward until it disappeared completely. Once he was fully transformed, he then let out a human scream. The long bushy eyebrows that grew down his face and tangled into the long silvery mustache and beard, were the only recognizable features that were still remaining.

There he stood, whoever he was, without a stitch of clothing on. Thankfully, his beard hid most of his body. He turned to Red and said, "Let me introduce myself, my boy. My name is Alexandros... Alexandros, the Great.

Now, be a good lad and get me my robe." He was pointing to the little room he had just come out of.

Red turned his gaze from the long-haired man, to the little room. That's when he saw the robe laying on the floor. The dog was laying on it a few minutes ago, which was why Red had not seen it. Red walked over and retrieved the robe. As he turned to give the robe to Alexandros, the door to the room started to close. Alexandros shouted. "No, don't let it close! We need it open!"

Quickly, Red grabbed the door tightly. When he did, he felt a little pinch in his hand. He pulled his hand back and noticed a long splinter, lodged into his palm.

He did not make a sound, for he knew his words could cause him trouble. Instead, he clenched his teeth, and made an, "ugh" sound.

"Come here, lad, let me have a look-see," Alexandros offered.

Red handed the robe to Alexandros first, then held out his hand, for assistance with the splinter.

"Maybe you should tell me your name, lad. Once I heal your hand, I will want to eat, not socialize. So go on with it, boy, what do people call you?"

Red did not answer. Instead, he just stared at the old man with the long silvery eyebrows and beard. He tried to mouth the words without using his voice, as if he were saying it, just without the sound.

"Ray? Your name is Ray?" Alexandros asked.

Shaking his head side to side rigorously signifying "no," Red tried again. This time he released his hand from Alexandros's grip. He bent down and used his fingers to write in the dust on the floor. After he wrote his name in the dust, Red looked up to Alexandros to see if he understood. By the look on his face, he did not.

Alexandros responded, with what looked like a hint of a smile "I am sorry my friend, but I cannot read that, unless your name is semicircle, half square, dash, circle, wavy line."

Red pointed to each symbol he drew and expected it to be obvious. Red did not realize that his writing was in a different language. He just knew it was the Bonk Bonk word for Red's name. Frustrated, Red stood up and exclaimed, "Red!"

Just as Red stated his name, the splinter in his hand began to flow with blood. Panic- stricken, he looked around the room, for something he could use to stop the bleeding.

"Quick, give me back your hand and relax, my boy."

Not sure what to do, or expect, Red extended his hand, once again, to Alexandros, who had already pushed up the sleeves to his robe and was now mumbling something to himself.

Alexandros took Red's hand into his left, and with his right hand hovering over Red's, he made small circular motions, all the while, still mumbling.

A few seconds later, the bleeding ceased and the splinter popped out of Red's hand like a cork popping out of a bottle. As it flew into the air, Alexandros caught it and put it into the pocket of his robe.

"Alexandros the Great.....at your service," said Alexandros proudly. "You know, my boy, that spell was the first bit of magic I have been able to perform for over twenty years. Suddenly frowning, he added, "Curse that wretched room."

Red looked toward the room and then back at Alexandros with a curious smile, still unsure of what to make of this old man. Even though he would love to ask him a thousand questions, he knew one thing was for sure, he was glad when the splinter popped out of his hand and glad it stopped bleeding. Still, Red wanted to talk to Alexandros, but he knew he could not. *If only there was a way to talk without speaking verbally. I've got it,* he thought. Red opened his mouth, but did not speak. Instead, he shook his head from side to side to signify "no," and then he pointed to his throat.

"What do you mean, you cannot speak? Red, I just heard you shout your name." He looked puzzled, and then he put the pieces together. "But then, that's when your hand started to bleed," stated Alexandros. "Oh I see," he said. "Do you mean to tell me, that if you speak aloud, something will happen?"

Excitedly, Red jumped up and down, shaking his head, gesturing a "yes!" He was so happy to be able to share his secret, without actually having to tell him, verbally.

Placing his hand on Red's shoulder, Alexandros said, "That's some great magic you have, my boy." Red stopped smiling for a moment and thought that was an odd thing to say in response, but he was too happy at the moment, to really think about it.

"Ok lad, let's see about something to eat. Are you hungry?" Alexandros asked, without waiting for an answer. He looked around the room and found the broken chair. He walked over to it, picked up the broken leg piece off the floor, held the two pieces together, and with a few muttered words under his breath, made the chair whole again. He placed the chair at the table and motioned for Red to sit down.

"Ah, now we are almost ready to eat," announced Alexandros. He reached down into the pocket of his robe and felt for his breakfast.

Chapter 5
The Room of Need

Red watched his new friend and wondered what he was doing. How was he going to make breakfast appear from his pockets? Red could always find some eggs, like he did this morning. As he watched Alexandros, Red reflected on all he had seen today. He had seen a large dog talk, and then watched, as it turned into a wizard. Next, he had witnessed a chair magically pieced back together. Now, he was watching Alexandros pick a crumb from his pocket, turn that into an entire loaf of bread, and heat it up with his fingers. He felt as though he had seen it all.

Now, sitting on a comfy chair, Red ate his nice, warm bread, while Alexandros walked around the room, eating his bread and telling of how he came to be in that tiny, cursed room.

"You see, lad, it was more than twenty years ago when I lived in a wondrous castle. I was the greatest wizard that Lanzeville had ever seen. Then one day, a young lass, came to me and begged me to rescue her beloved fiancé.

You see, she told me that while they were out riding, her and her fiancé stopped by a stream to water the horses. She decided to go off and explore the pretty woodlands, while he kept watch over the horses as they drank. On the way back to the stream, she heard a strange noise and hid behind a nearby bush. Without warning, a witch jumped out in front of her fiancé and started chanting something. Right before her eyes, the two of them were instantly, gone. She had figured that it must have been some sort of "Disappearing Spell". By then, she was crying and added that it was the last she saw of her beloved.

Fortunately for the lass, she had not been seen by the witch and was able to get away.

Of course, when she came straight over to the greatest wizard in Lanzeville and asked for assistance, I had to accept. Alexandros proudly extended his arms and bowed, as if to introduce himself again.

Alexandros stopped and asked Red if he was following along, or should he slow down. From the look on Red's face, he was clearly fascinated by the story and wanted to know more, in great detail.

"So, off I went, on what I later learned was a "Fool's Run", to find the young man. I transformed myself into an Irish wolfhound and tracked a scent down to this house very close to a stream. It looked abandoned, and the door was slightly opened so, I went in to take a look. Since there was only one room, and a closet, there weren't many places for anyone to hide, yet surprisingly, the door to the closet opened, and someone pushed me in. As the door closed behind me, it locked, and it denied my attempts to transform back into a man. I had to wait there until someone opened the door. That's when I realized the closet was, in fact, a Room of Need, and that there was never a witch, or a fiancé to rescue, in the first place. Apparently, I had been tricked by the young lass and whoever had sent her. Of course, at that point, all I knew is that it would take someone with great power to over-ride the power of the room. Alexandros was now looking distant and hurt at the same time, as if he now knew who was behind all of this.

Red's eyes were full of wonder as he listened to the amazing story that Alexandros was sharing with him. Red looked puzzled because he could not yet completely comprehended what Alexandros had just said. Red pointed to himself, and drew his eyebrows tightly together. He did not understand why Alexandros had said, "someone with great power." He did not have great power. Yes, he could make things happen when he spoke, he knew that was a fact. But Alexandros can make things happen too. He is a wizard. Surely he is more powerful than himself.

"Yes, my boy, you are more powerful. You cannot verbally talk to me for fear of what it might do. That is powerful. Your mere words could do someone harm," said Alexandros, trying to explain.

Red now pointed to Alexandros, to signify that he, too, could use mere words to manipulate objects.

"No, my boy, my words are in spell form. They are spells that I must master prior to using. For any wizard worth his salt, would never use a spell, until it was ready. If you are not a master of your craft, it could backfire on you," Alexandros explained.

Red turned away from Alexandros, and pointed to the Room of Need. Alexandros was getting really good at figuring out Red's expressions and gestures, because he knew immediately, that Red wanted to know more about the Room of Need.

"You see, the one who locked me into that tiny wretched room, well, their need was far greater than mine. So there, I remained, as a prisoner. While I was in there and no one else was around, my need to stay alive was the only need left, so it kept me alive."

As Alexandros finished his tale, Red finished his bread.

"Now that I am back to my old self, I do believe I will track down the treacherous fool, who locked me into that Room of Need," said Alexandros. Continuously pacing the room, he added, "What about you, Red, whatever could have led you here, my boy?"

It seemed that Alexandros did not want to waste any time standing still, since the past twenty years had been spent lying on a cold floor.

Red, being unable to converse freely, wasn't that interested in small talk but only wanted to ask which way led him home. Actually, he would even be fine if he knew where he was now and then he could figure out his own way home. But how could he communicate that to Alexandros without words? He stood up and walked over to the Room of Need and stood in the doorway. He looked over his shoulder to Alexandros, and pointed once more. Then, Red motioned with both hands for Alexandros to stay where he was and to watch. On a hunch, Red conjured up thoughts of his village, making his need more powerful than anything he has ever wanted in his life. He was hoping that if this room works off the greatest need, then it should show him his village. He desperately missed his village and his family, so he concentrated on his own hut, as well as the pitch black school hut. He pictured in his mind, all the elders who stood in front of him, chanting their tribal name.

The image of his village was crystal clear in his mind and his need so great, that the walls in the Room of Need began to change, just as he had hoped. Alexandros stepped closer, amazed at what he was watching. Red became very excited to see the trees of his village taking shape right before his eyes.

Red saw his village as clear as day on the walls of this Room of Need. This was no memory, but an actual, clear picture of what was happening right at that very moment. It was as if he was standing above the village looking down upon it. Each wall represented a different part of the village that was familiar to him. On one wall, he could see the elders around a fire and their huts. On another wall, he saw the school hut and the children playing near it. On yet another wall, he saw his father, his brothers and his sisters all down at the seaside fishing, not far from the village. As the walls began to reveal more of his village, Red looked at Alexandros, who was now standing next to him. He was smiling at Red, who was pointing to himself and then to the village that they were seeing on the walls of The Room of Need.

"Incredible," said Alexandros. "That is your home? It looks lovely. Why did you leave?"

Red shook his head slowly, anger swelling inside of him. He wanted to tell Alexandros that he did not leave and that he was summoned out of his village by the elders and his mother's spirit. He wanted to tell him that she came to him and sent him on this journey, because the elders thought it was time for Red to be a man. He suddenly felt sad that he was not home. He missed his village terribly. He wanted to be home now.

Unfortunately, with his thoughts becoming unfocused, the room started to change again, causing the village to become blurry. At this point, Red could no longer make out the members of his tribe or his family any longer, so he turned toward Alexandros, and with tears in his eyes, he turned his back on the Room of Need. He did not see the walls now starting to display a picture of a map. He did not see that next it had changed to trails which showed the exact directions home. No... Red did not see that at all. All he could see was a blur from the tears that were now streaming down his face. He closed the door behind him and ran out of the little house, away from Alexandros.

During that same time, Alexandros also had his eyes on the Room of Need while it was still showing the Bonk Bonk village. He, too, had missed the part where the map appeared because when Red became upset, Alexandros had noticed Red losing his concentration, and turned to check on his friend. Of course, Red was already running out of the cottage.

Sadly, neither of them noticed that the room walls had changed and now, neither of them will ever know the Room of Need had tried to show Red the way home.

Chapter 6
Attack of the Lady Bugs

Alexandros ran after Red, who was walking as fast as he could, away from the little house.

"Red", Alexandros called out trying to catch up to him. "How about I help you find your way home? Once you are back in your quaint little village, I shall continue to hunt down my captor. How does that sound?" Alexandros asked, while attempting to give Red a reassuring smile that was hidden behind his long mustache.

It was a long time before Red stopped walking. He did not know where he was walking to. He was not sure where he was, or, which way would lead him home. He just knew that standing in the little house was not going to get him anywhere. Red finally stopped and let out a defeated sigh. He looked to the sky above, searching for an answer that was not there.

Alexandros spoke up, "Twenty years ago, I was on my way to the river, which then led me to that house back there. So, that means there should be a river nearby. Maybe we could retrace my steps and at the same time look for things that may help, too."

Alexandros looked to Red for his response, and when he looked at him, he appeared to be frozen. Red was bent over at the waist with his hands on his knees, his head turned toward a cluster of bushes on his right. Alexandros turned his gaze to see what Red was staring at. It turned out to be an extremely large hand. The fingers were at least six feet long, with the palm of the hand just as long.

Red stood transfixed as Alexandros walked over to the hand, and then creeped through the bushes to see what lay beyond. As Red stood there waiting for Alexandros to return, he heard footsteps behind him. Turning quickly, he saw nothing. Not sure if he really did hear something, or someone, Red continued to look cautiously at the surrounding trees and bushes. Once more from behind him, Red heard quick-paced footsteps. It sounded like three or four quick steps, then it stopped, then three or four more steps, then it stopped again. Red was now on high alert from some unseen foe. He thought that now would be good time to look for a weapon. He searched the ground for a broken branch or a rock he could throw. Seeing nothing, he decided to make a run for it through the cluster of bushes in an attempt to find Alexandros.

Once Red made it through the bushes, he stopped dead in his tracks. What he saw had made his jaw drop. He was standing in front of the largest eyeball he had ever seen. It was not just an eyeball, of course, but part of an entire body. It was the first giant Red had ever seen.

When Red was able to move, he side- stepped slowly out of view from the enormous blue eye. As he walked away from the head and down to the neck and shoulders of the giant, Red walked into a vine that was suspended in the air. He noticed that the giant was tied down. He also saw that the vines extended across the giant's chest and continued all the way to his feet. *There must be thousands of vines holding him down,* he thought. Red began to feel sorry for the giant. *What could he have done to deserve to be restrained?*

As he walked towards the giant's feet, maneuvering through the vines, searching for Alexandros. He did not think the giant would have been able to make a meal out of him since his head was tied down, as well as his arms. Frantically, Red picked up the pace as he continued his search for Alexandros. When Red came to the giant's knees, he thought he heard Alexandros yelling for him. Red ran around to the other side of the giant's feet. He was shocked to see Alexandros fighting off a group of what could be best described as four-foot-tall ladybugs.

They had four legs and two antennae. They were mostly black, with a dark purple hue on their backs. There were quite a few of them attacking Alexandros, who appeared to have no visible weapon to fend them off. Then Red saw lightning shoot from Alexandros's fingertips, striking three ladybugs simultaneously, and then branching off to two other ladybugs. It seemed that if the ladybugs were within two or three feet of each other, they would each get a branch of the lightning. Red ran towards the fight, not knowing what he was going to use as a weapon. He looked for a stick or a rock, but again there was nothing around. Alexandros now reached into his robes and pulled out a sliver of wood. It was the same splinter that Alexandros removed from Red's hand. Alexandros instantly turned it into a staff and threw it to Red, he wasted no time joining the fight.

There were ladybugs jumping in the air, attempting to kick Red in the head, but once they were airborne, he hit their shells with his staff and knocked them off their course. He jumped around swinging his staff, trying to simultaneously stay away from Alexandros's lightning strikes. He thought it would hurt a lot especially since he did not have a protective shell like the lady bugs did. He knew the flashes of lightning were not fatal, since the ladybugs just bounced away, then resumed their attack. Two of the ladybugs now joined together to form a ball and tried to crash into Red and Alexandros. They caught on pretty quickly, and would either side-step the rolling ladybugs or jump over them.

There was a rolling ladybug about to strike at Red. He jumped onto its back and used that momentum to leap forward to attack another cluster of ladybugs that were attacking Alexandros. At the same time that Red was jumping in the air, Alexandros had shot lightning from his fingertip to the oncoming cluster of ladybugs. Red struck the ladybugs and knocked them away from his friend, but then he caught the full force of the lightning, right to his chest. He fell hard to the ground, unconscious.

With no time to check on Red, Alexandros needed to even the odds. He was alone now and fighting what seemed like an endless battle. Instead of shooting the lightning at the oncoming ladybugs, he suddenly realized that he had another ally. So now Alexandros began shooting the lightning at the vines holding down the giant. Next, he ran to Red, using his own body as a shield to protect Red from the vines that were beginning to snap and burn away.

Once the giant realized he was not tied down, he sat up, pulling the broken restraints off of him. When he threw them off his large frame, a few of the ladybugs became caught up in the vines and were cast aside too. The rest began to scatter in all directions as they realized that their prize was now released.

Red was sprawled out on the ground, lying on his back. He slowly began to open his eyes and started to sit up. Alexandros sat back no longer needing to protect him.

"Are you okay, lad?" He asked Red, who was looking puzzled.

When he sat up his head felt dizzy, unsure if he would be able to stand. Red did not think the magic Alexandros was producing would hurt as much as it did because for the ladybugs, it only seemed to knock them off their feet, maybe even just stun them for a split second.

Red was not sure how long he had been unconscious. But he knew he had to snap out of it, now that there was an extremely large person sitting in front of him, who also looked confused.

Alexandros stood next to him, his glare transfixed at the newly- released giant. Red was not sure what scared him more, the size of the giant or the fact that he looked confused.

"Shall we make a new friend?" Alexandros asked Red. He turned to Red and helped him to stand. Red nodded back to him, and they both walked slowly toward the giant.

Alexandros began to speak loudly enough so that he could be heard.

"Hello up there! Might we offer our appreciation for your assistance!"

After being tied down for who knows how long, Red hoped the giant was not hungry. It would be a horrible end to an already unpleasant day, if they were to be eaten by a giant, especially after all that they had been through.

Chapter 7
Thug

"Hello there my enormous friend," Alexandros said a little louder. "Thank you for your assistance in that scuffle." He began to walk away from Red, so that the giant would see him better. He stood standing next to the giant's hand that was now resting on the ground.

Although the giant was looking around, he did not see Alexandros, who was now yelling up to him and repeating his introduction for a third time. When the giant finally looked down it was because there was a little man standing there poking his hand with a stick. Once the giant looked down and turned his head quizzically to the side, Alexandros threw aside the stick. He did not want to seem aggressive.

"Start waving," he said to Red quickly.

Red did as he was instructed, and as he waved he watched the giant. *He looks young for such a large person,* Red thought. The giant did not have any facial hair like Alexandros did, no beard, no mustache. Instead, he had a boyish, round face.

He also noticed the giant was dressed in what could be considered boys clothing, blue shorts and a red shirt. His blonde hair was filled with twigs and grass from being restrained to the ground.

Alexandros stopped waving and asked, "What's your name? My name is Alexandros, and this is Red." The boy giant responded by pointing to his chest and said in a deep thunderous voice,

"Me, Thug."

"Thug, you say? That's a mighty name for a mighty boy," Alexandros responded.

"Huh huh huh…huh huh huh," Thug chuckled.

Red, who was no longer waving, looked nervously at Thug. He was not sure if what he heard was a laugh. It was very deep and made the ground rumble. Could that be a smile on Thug's face, or the expression of a hungry giant, just before he eats a snack?

Thug watched the man with the facial hair.

"You name Al-dros?" he asked Alexandros.

Thug reached out with his enormous hand. It looked as though he was going to shake Alexandros's hand in greeting. Instead, Thug picked up Alexandros and brought him to his chest and hugged him. Once Thug had finished his embrace and lowered his hand, Alexandros looked limp and his eyes were closed in Thug's large hands.

"Al-dros tired," said Thug. "Al-dros need sleepy time."

Thug put Alexandros down on the ground so that he could rest. Red rushed over to Alexandros and was trying to revive his unconscious friend. Red shook his shoulders trying to wake him, but when that did not work, he began to slap Alexandros in the face. Finally, Alexandros started coughing and opened his eyes.

"Alright, Red, you can stop hitting me!" he said between coughing fits. Red grabbed Alexandros and embraced him when he realized he was alright.

"I'm ok, I just couldn't breathe. He was crushing me."

Red stood up, extended his hand to Alexandros and helped him to stand. Once they were both standing, Red felt a huge push on his back which made him fall forward. When he fumbled forward he landed with his face in the dirt. Angrily, he stood up and brushed the dirt from his mouth and face. He turned to see Thug kneeling and leaning forward. He had one hand extended and he was pointing at Red. That's when Red realized that Thug had used his finger to knock him to the ground. Alexandros, seeing that Red's face was seething with anger, stepped between Thug's finger and Red. Looking at Red, Alexandros said,

"I think he knocked you down so that he could help you up, like you helped me."

He turned and looked up at Thug,

"Is that right, Thug? You wanted to help him? You wanted to show him that you would help him if he needed it?" He asked Thug while shaking his head up and down, trying to give him the correct answer.

"Thank you, my friend." Alexandros said to Thug.

He reached with both hands and shook Thug's large finger.

Thug began to smile. He looked at Red and said,

"You name Red. Thug shirt red. You name Red, Thug shirt....huh huh huh huh...."

Thug apparently thought Red's name was funny.

Red was now getting angrier and wanted Thug to know it. First, he was attacked by purple ladybugs trying to help him. Then, he was pushed to the ground by a giant, his way of saying thank you. Now, he was being laughed at because of his name. He had enough of this giant kid. He shouted loud enough for the giant to hear him:

"QUIET YOU FOOL!"

Just then, Thug's laughter stopped in mid chuckle. He was no longer laughing at Red or his name. He looked frightened that he was no longer making any sound at all. He went from kneeling down looking at the two men, to standing up and throwing a silent temper tantrum. He was stomping his feet up and down, panic taking over since he was unable to cry out. His hands grasping at his throat, he began pulling at his neck trying to pull out the sound.

"Get out of the way!" hollered Alexandros, running away from Thug's stomping feet. He and Red ran toward a cluster of trees, hoping it would shelter them. Once a safe distance away Alexandros said, "Stay here."

Red did just that. He hid behind a tree and waited for Alexandros.

Chapter 8
Thug's Story

Alexandros stepped a few feet away from Red, arms outstretched in front of him. He began to conjure a spell, his mouth moving faster than his hands. He took a step, waving one hand clockwise, while moving the other counter-clockwise. Alexandros took another step forward then stopped, simultaneously reciting the spell. As the spell progressed, Thug began to move slower and slower. Everyone and everything else moved in real time. Only Thug's movements were beginning to freeze. Even though Red could hear the words Alexandros chanted, it sounded like gibberish to him.

It was amazing to watch a giant move so slowly, and then become frozen in space and time. Seeing that the danger of Thug's stomping feet had passed, Red ran over to the wizard.

"I have made the air around him very thick. It slows his movements, but it will not hold him long. Still concentrating on his spell, Alexandros said to Red, "You frightened him by taking his voice. You must allow him to speak again,"

He did not want to be teased by Thug again, but Red knew Alexandros was right. Thug must be allowed to speak again.

"Let's have it. I cannot hold him much longer. He is too large," warned Alexandros.

Red could see that Alexandros was struggling to keep the spell holding Thug. Reluctantly, Red spoke softly, "Thug, speak." Looking irritated, as if he were just scolded by a parent, Red walked quickly back to the trees for safety.

Almost immediately, Thug's voice returned and he began to scream again. His movements were still slow but his voice was in real time. For the second time, Red was hearing words that were separated from mouth movements. The first time was when he saw his mother during the smoke filled reunion.

I wonder which is worse, a giant child who doesn't know his own strength, or a scared giant about to be set free. Red knew he was about to find out and neither sounded choice sounded better than the other.

It was time for Alexandros to reverse his spell. In order for it to work, he must recite his spell in the exact way he had cast it, but now, completely backwards. His hands must flow perfectly, twisting and turning in the opposite directions. This was not something all wizards could do easily. It takes a long time to master, but Alexandros was truly a skilled wizard.

Slowly, Thug's movements became what they should be. He started to move quicker than he had been previously moving, and before long he was back in normal speed. Alexandros began explaining to Thug that Red was upset, and that he did not mean to frighten him and take away his voice.

"Thug, please sit down." Alexandros requested.

As Thug sat, something snapped under his feet. Red noticed it was not a twig, but a full grown tree. Once he sat down, Thug had tried to make himself comfortable. He reached under his bottom, and then retrieved a boulder. He tossed it aside like one would toss an apple core when finished eating. The boulder was not seen again, although, you could hear it crashing through the trees as it lost its momentum and stopped somewhere off in the distance.

Alexandros approached the giant and spoke slowly so that he was sure Thug would understand.

"Thug, it's ok. We are not going to hurt you."

A look of understanding spread on Thug's face.

"Thug like Al-dros and Red," Thug said, in his deep voice.

Red smiled at the way Thug was pronouncing Alexandros's name. He suddenly realized that Thug was nothing more than a child in a humongous body, and that he should not get upset with him again so quickly.

Casually glancing around, Red saw apples in the nearby trees. After the recent excitement, Red realized that he was hungry again. He felt his stomach growl in search of food. He walked up to a tree but the fruit was hanging just out of reach. Red tried jumping up to get fruit in hand. He squatted down and thrust his body up into the air; his arms flailing around trying to get his prize. When his arms and legs were stretched out, he resembled a frog in mid leap. Red heard laughter coming from Thug and had automatically assumed that he was the source of Thug's amusement, again.

After watching Red for a few minutes, Thug reached over without straining and tore a branch from the tree. He then set it down at Red's feet and smiled. Red was now sweating and panting heavily from all his jumping. He stood there and watched as Thug ripped off another branch and took a bite from it. Thug sat there mindlessly chewing the fruit, leaves and tree bark. Red laughed to himself as he picked an apple off the newly accessible branch and ate it.

"See that, he's helping you," Alexandros said approvingly.

Alexandros walked over to Red and the tree branch, picked an apple, and ate it. Thug, feeling very pleased with himself, looked at Alexandros, and smiled.

As he ate his delicious fruit, Alexandros looked to Thug and asked, "When we found you, you were tied up. What happened?"

Looking quite sad, Thug began to tell his story as if Alexandros had brought up a bad memory.

"Thug home," he pointed up toward the sky. Then while mimicking the movements of a butterfly, Thug continued, "Thug play, find pretty. Thug want pretty. Pretty go to up-down. Now Thug imitated his mother by pointing his finger at Alexandros and said, "Mom of Thug say 'no fall." At this, he hung his head downward in sadness.

"Thug, what is an up-down?" Alexandros asked.

"Thug go down and Thug go up." He explained while he pointed upward again.

"Up where?"

"Mom of Thug be sad. Thug fall."

"It's ok Thug, she won't be mad at you. Now, when you say you fell, what does that mean?" Alexandros asked.

"Thug home up."

"Do you mean you live up above the clouds?" Alexandros asked, pointing up to the sky where a cluster of clouds were.

Thug smiled and nodded his head. He was happy now that they knew where he came from.

"Thug see pretty. Pretty go to up-down."

Perplexed, Alexandros asked Thug, "What is an up-down?"

"Thug go up, and Thug go down," Thug explained, impatiently.

"You mean it's your way up to your home and down here to our land?"

Thug was starting to look confused. This was too much conversation than he could handle. He just shrugged his shoulders. He looked from Alexandros then to Red, who was sitting on the broken tree limb eating and listening to Thug's simple mind at work. After Red ate his third apple, he stood up and walked around. He looked up to the sky and wondered; *how is it possible that someone could live above the clouds?*

Thug continued, "Up-down many colors. Thug not see up-down now." He was sadly looking slowly in every direction.

"I think I have it! You use a rainbow to go up and down. That's miraculous!" said Alexandros.

Red, still looking up to the sky, realized he was no longer looking for a house in the clouds, but was now looking for a rainbow. *If Thug needed to ride a rainbow to go home, what does he do when there are no rainbows?*

Alexandros plucked an apple from the downed tree branch. He bit into it until he was able to extract the seeds. He slid the seeds into his pocket and then finished his second apple. He walked up to Thug.

"Thug, we can help you find your way home. Do not fret. Tell me. I am curious. Why did those ladybugs tie you up?"

Thug looked to Alexandros, still looking rather sad about not finding a way home. He said,

"Thug fall. Thug see ball. Thug want ball. Ball hurt Thug."

Red was thinking of Thug's simple mind and trying to piece together the story. He could not imagine a giant falling to the ground and no one feeling the earthquake it would have caused. He wondered if there was some sort of spell on the giant to stop him from causing damage when he was exploring the lower land. As for the purple ball, well that could have been the swarm of ladybugs flying. They must have noticed a giant following them, and Thug must have gotten frightened. Red remembered how nervous he was when he first met Thug, too.

"I see, so the ball you followed was actually the ladybugs. They broke flying formation, then turned and attacked you out of fear," Alexandros said after analyzing the situation.

As Thug kept looking at the sky above, his eyes were filling with tears of worry. It looked, to Red, like Thug was beginning to cry.

"Easy now, Thug. We will help you find a way home," Alexandros said, trying to offer some sympathetic words. Unfortunately, it did not seem to comfort Thug at all. He was just getting more and more upset.

"Thug want home," he said to the two little people watching him cry into his giant hands.

Red was feeling sorry for this huge little boy. He wanted to do what he could to help. So he walked over to Thug's enormous knees, grabbed a handful of blue shorts, and began to climb up the giant. Red had made it to the giant's stomach when Thug reached down and scooped him up in his massive hands. Red fell backwards against them and then he steadied himself as best as he could.

Red repeatedly moved his arms diagonally up and down. His intention was to get the giant to lift his hand up higher. He needed a clear view of the sky.

*I may not know **my** way home, but, I do know where **you** live,* Red thought.

Chapter 9
Snars

"What are you up to lad?" Alexandros yelled from the ground.

Red felt the hand that was supporting him move suddenly. He braced himself by throwing his arms out for balance. In the next moment he was being thrown forward. *What is he doing*? Red thought.

When Thug moved, Red began to slide off the huge hand. Quickly, he grabbed onto the enormous thumb at the last second. Red's feet were dangling as he hung above the ground just twenty feet below. He held on as tight as he could and thanked the sweet spirits that his own arms were long enough to make it around the appendage. Red had noticed the size of Thug's hands, but since he was a giant, he thought everything on Thug should be large. Now that he was this close and personal to Thug's thumb, Red thought the giant's hands were his largest feature. At this moment Red was glad for it. If they were any smaller he would have already fallen to his death.

"Huh...huh...huh, you funny," Thug said. Then Red felt his body being lifted. He was set down next to

Alexandros on Thug's other hand. With his eyes and mouth wide open, Red looked at Alexandros with a look of shock and surprise. Thug must have bent over to pick up Alexandros with his other hand, and that caused Red to almost fall.

"Close your mouth, boy, or the birds will come and nest on your tongue," Alexandros said, with a bit of a laugh.

"Huh huh... huh huh, birds." Thug laughed and sprayed saliva all over Red and Alexandros.

"Ewww," Red groaned as he wiped the saliva from his face and arms.

"If you make him laugh any more, we will drown," Alexandros cautioned, still smiling and obviously not bothered by the heavy saliva that was saturating his robes.

"You know, lad, although I do have the ability to make a rain cloud, it looks like there are already rain clouds up yonder. Yet my magic may still be needed. Look over there," Alexandros instructed, as he pointed westward. There were storm clouds beginning to form. "If we can make it westward before the rain falls, I can make us a rainbow."

"Up-down?" Thug was excited and smiling at the thought of going home. Red could understand wanting to go home and not knowing how to get there. Sadness filled Red's heart. He wanted to be home with his family. He missed fishing with his brothers. He missed his sisters cooking the daily catch. He even missed his father, though he hated to admit it. Red closed his eyes, remembering the day that he had went hunting with his father.

The day started off great with a wonderful father-son hunt, but, after a few hours of hiding in the shrubbery, Red had fallen asleep. How could he resist when it was so comfortable lying down on the cool earth, with the sounds of nature all about. He just could not help himself. When he woke up after dark, his father was nowhere in sight. At first, Red thought his father was still hiding nearby, so he waited. After a few hours of waiting, Red decided he should make his way home. Luckily, Red knew the layout of the woods and how to get home. When he returned to the village, Red noticed his father sitting near the fire, eating his prize. Red learned two valuable lessons that day. First, never fall asleep while hunting. Second, if you sleep through dinner, do not expect there to be anything left over.

His thoughts snapped back to present time. He was now sitting on a six foot long hand, next to a wizard, suspended more than twenty feet in the air. All Red wanted, was to not fall. Thug's hand may be the largest he had ever seen, but with two people sitting on it, it suddenly felt a little small.

Once again, Red felt Thug's hand move and nervously, Red hooked arms with Alexandros.

"Easy now, lad, look there!" he said, as he tilted his head. Red blinked repeatedly, putting his memory of home aside. He looked to the west and noticed a heavy patch of dark gray clouds. He knew Thug's long strides could close the distance from here to there rather quickly. They would be able to look for a rain cloud and even a possible rainbow.

Thug lifted his hand so that Red and Alexandros were at his eye level and said,

"Thug go home now. You make up- down?" With a quizzical look on his face, he waited for a response. Alexandros looked back at the eyes that were bigger than his own head and said,

"Thug, I promise you, we will get you home."

"Yaaaay," Thug said, as he closed his fingers and raised his hands above his head and cheered. He seemed to have forgotten he had two passengers in his left hand. When screams could be heard from above Thug's head, he decided to lower his still-clenched hands. Alexandros and Red were now a jumbled mess of intertwined body parts.

"Thug sorry," he said, as he opened his hands and cupped them together, giving the two travelers plenty of room to separate. Red now felt as though he were closer to Alexandros, in more ways than one. He suddenly wished he had on longer animal skins. His tribal skins were cut down to his knee, but once you are intertwined with another man while on an over-sized hand, you feel as though they would never be long enough.

Once Red had some room to breathe, he tried to relax. He was getting the feeling that he would always have to be on guard in the presence of the unpredictable giant.

Red looked to the ground below as Thug walked. He watched all the treetops beneath him. From this height, they looked like broccoli crowns. While Thug was walking, Red once again wondered why he never heard any trees crunching below or felt the earth tremble with the weight of Thugs massive body. He wondered again if there was some sort of enchantment on him. *How can this giant roam the ground and no one ever know?*

In less time than one could have imagined, their destination had been reached. They saw a break in the clouds where the sun was peeking through with all its might. Just then Red heard whistling. It was a beautiful melody and he noticed that it was coming from Alexandros, who stood there with his eyes closed, his head tilted toward the heavens and his hands cupped to the sides of his mouth to amplify the sound.

"Thug, stop. We wait here," Alexandros exclaimed, as he searched the ground below.

Red looked to Alexandros, curiously.

"I have summoned the Snars. They will help," Alexandros said, as if Red should know what he meant.

Red had never heard of Snars, nor did he know what they were going to help with. There was nothing for him to do but wait and see.

Within a few minutes, Red heard more whistling. He looked again to Alexandros. He was smiling and looking at the trees below. "Here they come…look, lads," said Alexandros, pointing to the oncoming swarm.

The Snars flew up and stopped just a few feet from Alexandros and Red. Thug's facial expression showed that he was more than a little nervous. His eyebrows squeezed together and his lips clenched tight.

"Do not fret, my large friend. They are not the ladybugs. They will not attack you. They are here to make your up-down" Alexandros said, and then turned to the Snars to greet them. "Hello, my little ones. Thank you for heeding my call. We need your assistance."

As Alexandros explained the situation to the Snars, Red tried to grasp what he was looking at. Never in all his days had he seen such creatures.

They were less than three inches tall and each one a different color. Their bodies resembled that of a small turtle, with their narrow, serpent-like heads and necks. Their arms and legs were that of an aquatic turtle, with webbed hands and feet. The major difference was in the humanistic facial features. They had eyes, a nose and mouth like a human. Their ears were just a tiny hole on either side of their heads, and each Snar had an antenna coming from the top its tiny head.

While Alexandros continued to speak to the Snars, some of them were still whistling. Red could see that their mouths did not move and that the music came from their antennae.

Red's thoughts turned quickly to his family. He wondered if anyone was missing him the way that he was missing them. He also wondered, *what was the point of finding my way home, if I could never explain to the villagers what wonderful sights I have seen, and all the wonderful creatures I have come across. When was the last time they saw a vibrantly-colored, humanoid turtle whistling through an antenna?* He smiled to himself as he pushed the village out of his thoughts and concentrated on what he was seeing now.

He looked at the incredible array of colors before him and thought he knew what Alexandros was planning.

Chapter 10
Snar-bow

When Alexandros finished speaking to the Snars, he turned back to Red and Thug, to explain.

"I have asked the Snars to help us. That darkest blue Snar over there is their leader, Tiddle-toa, and the pink one next to him is his mate, Slo-zo. They have all agreed to band together and form the necessary rainbow. Their shells are made of the hardest material I have ever come across so, together they can make a Snar-rainbow strong enough for Thug to ascend."

Without waiting for a response, Alexandros turned towards Tiddle-toa and whistled again. Tiddle-toa hovered closer to Alexandros and Red, and then whistled a response from his antenna. It was a sound more like a trumpeter waking soldiers for their morning reveille, although this time, the tune was higher in pitch, and longer in note.

In a matter of minutes, multi-colored Snars from all over the forest began to fly towards the awaiting group. From below, the trees and grass seemed to lose their color. The tulips beneath them seemed less yellow, red and orange. The tree trunks looked less brown, and the grass was now a dull green. Thug seemed startled by the onrush of colors. He took a step back and made an attempt to shield his tiny friends, using his free hand to cover Red and Alexandros. Once again, they became a jumble of flesh in the darkness of his oversized hands.

Before long, there were thousands and thousands of Snars hovering before Thug. They kept a safe distance so as not to alarm him any further. Seemingly aware that their sheer numbers scared Thug, they began to create a visual that he could trust. A hundred yellow Snars formed a large circle, and then ten of the blue Snars created two smaller circles of five and placed themselves in the top of the yellow circle. Finally, a group of red Snars, moved into position to form a semi-circle smile at the bottom. Together, they had created a very large smiling face. To calm Thug's nerves, they began to whistle a happy cheerful song. For such a large boy, he sure was easily scared by small creatures.

"Look, Aldros. Thug see pretty," he announced, as he removed his hands from covering Alexandros and Red. He stretched out his hand so that they could get a closer view.

"Yes, I see, I see. Look over there, Thug. They are building another pretty for you," Alexandros said pointing off in the distance.

"Again, again, make pretty," begged Thug.

The Snars that had formed the smiley face, started to separate and became one with the rainbow that was now taking shape.

While the Snars were hard at work forming the rainbow, Alexandros began to tell Red about them.

"You know, it is very exciting to respond to a wizard's call. The Snars have the power to refuse, yet they came to me faster than any familiar I have ever called. A familiar you see, is a living being that a wizard can summon to do his bidding. In time, the spell expires and the familiar is set free. Snars, on the other hand, will stay with the wizard until the task is complete, or when they choose to leave.

They take such pride in blending in with the scenery so that passers-by do not realize they are there. The Snars go about their daily lives adding color to the forest, just like paint is used for a house, although Snars are far more vibrant. You might walk past a few hundred Snars and never be the wiser."

Red had watched when the Snars made the smiley face for Thug. Now they were forming a solid rainbow right before his eyes. What an amazing sight it was. Starting from the bottom was the violet, next was the indigo, then the blue, and then the green. The green was as green as the sharpest blade of grass. In fact, if blades of grass could be jealous, they surely would be after seeing this. Next was the yellow, then the orange, and finally red, which was so bright it made the shiniest looking apples look pale in comparison.

Since this was no ordinary rainbow forming before them, Red and his companions could also see the magnificent set of stairs forming on the narrow side of the rainbow. Looking directly at the broad side, you could not see it, but if you turned the rainbow to the narrow end you would see the stairs leading up into the clouds.

Red opened his eyes wide as he pointed to the incredible sight so that Thug would look, too.

"Thug see up-down!"

Red was suddenly nervous that Thug might start clapping his hands at any moment.

"Yes, Thug, we see the up-down too," Alexandros said approvingly.

"Yaaaay!," said Thug in a long exaggerated cheer. He was about to throw his hands in the air when he stopped awkwardly.

"NO THUG!" Alexandros shouted, while standing firm and pointing a strong hand at him, like a parent would do when scolding a child. Red reflexively crouched down and threw his arms over his head.

"Huh huh…huh…..huh, just kidding," Thug said sheepishly, as he lowered his hands.

"I think he likes it," Alexandros said mockingly. Suddenly turning serious, he told Red, "Now for the true test. Let's see if it takes Thug home."

Chapter 11
Going Up

One foot at a time, Thug stepped up onto the Snar rainbow and began ascending the obscure staircase. Red looked cautiously over the side of Thug's large hand. He wondered if the Snar rainbow would hold all their weight or if they would all crash to the ground.

"Easy now, Red, you wouldn't want to fall from this height," Alexandros said, as he put a hand on Red's shoulder.

"Thug go home now, see mom of Thug!" said Thug, excitedly

"Yes Thug, easy now, that's right, keep going up the steps, good lad," coaxed Alexandros.

Red looked ahead instead of down. Like a blind man who could now see, he felt like he was discovering each color for the first time.

If you have ever seen a rainbow from a distance, then you know how beautiful they are; but seeing a Snar rainbow is like looking at the purest form of each color. Red had never seen anything that could compare to this magnificent Snar rainbow, more easily called a Snar-bow.

Alexandros had said previously, that there is nothing stronger than a Snar's shell. So far, that has proven true. Thug ascended the stairs without any difficulty. With every step, the three of them went higher and higher, yet even with the enormous weight of the giant, the Snar-bow held firm and strong. Thug continued to carry his travel companions to his home, and the stairs underneath him did not shudder or shake.

As they reached the top of this amazingly colorful staircase created by humanoid turtles, they were about to cross the threshold to a giant's world, while being carried by a giant. Red was thinking that he could never have dreamed up such an adventure. A whistling sound tore him from his thoughts. Alexandros was once again, talking to the Snars. Red assumed it was a 'thank you' for their assistance. Since Red also wanted to show his gratitude, he joined in by smiling and waving to the Snars.

Once they reached the top, and were now in Thug's home world, Red saw large dome-like stone houses. As for the ground, he did not know what Thug was standing on. He could not tell if it was grass or dirt. All he could see was a thin layer of clouds, billowing around. There were a few houses scattered here and there. Yet, it was a dull sight with no colorful trees, no array of flowers, no green grass, and definitely not any wildlife running about. Red could now understand why Thug liked to come down to the land below. Even though Thug had a very simple mind, he was drawn to all the colors and textures the world below provided.

Just then a large woman, much taller than Thug, came running forward. She swept him up into her large arms and embraced him.

"Me son, me son is home!" She repeated, as she spun him around, and then hugged him again. As quickly as he was picked up, Thug closed his hands around Alexandros and Red to prevent them from being thrown. When Meme finally let go of her son, Thug held out his hand to his mother.

"Mom of Thug, this Thug friend, Aldros," he said pointing to Alexandros. "This Red, huh huh…huh huh, he funny," Thug said, pointing to Red.

Red waved a cautious greeting to Thug's mother.

"Hello, Madam," said Alexandros.

"Hello friend of Thug. Me name Meme. Meme want food, come."

Thug's mother turned and walked away towards her stone house with Thug following close behind.

All the houses looked like they could come crashing down easily. Red carefully viewed the other homes in the giant land, all looking hastily built. It seemed too difficult for a giant to grasp the concept of a well-constructed house. Half-way through building their home, they probably forgot what they were doing and then thought that they were putting the boulders in a large pile.

When they crossed the threshold to the house, Red saw two crudely cut trees lying on their side, with branches and bark stripped from it. He assumed this was their sitting room. The next room that Thug brought them into was the kitchen. It had a stone fire pit. It also had two smaller tree stumps for sitting, with a large tree block that served as their dining table.

Meme went over to the stone fireplace and pulled a pan of rolls from it. Red could smell their sweetness and his mouth began to water. Thug walked over to the table and put his hand down so that Red and Alexandros could step onto the surface. Red feared for a moment, that Meme might be under the impression that he and Alexandros were meant as a snack along with the rolls. He pushed the gruesome thought from his mind, and decided to trust that Thug would protect him should Meme decide to make a crunchy treat out of them.

"Thug, what is that over there?" Alexandros asked, while pointing to the only other item in the room. It seemed oddly out of place. The furnishings of Thug and Meme's home were easily constructed and simple. This, on the other hand, was elaborate and beautiful. An exquisite cage made from intertwining twigs, hung down from a tree branch that was stuck between the rock crevices.

"Huh... huh huh...that Nonie house. She Thug friend."

Thug took a roll from the pan and placed it on the table for Alexandros and Red. "You eat now," he said.

Wasting no time, Red immediately began to pull off pieces from the large roll; which was almost as tall as him. He began stuffing his face until he was full, not caring how hot the roll was and apparently not aware of how hungry he really was. Completely oblivious to his surroundings, Red did not even notice where Alexandros was at the time. There was nothing in his mind except for this large, sweet, delicious roll.

Red finished devouring as much as his stomach could handle. When he had nothing left but a small chunk of bread in his hand, he finally noticed that Alexandros was talking to an attractive woman. Suddenly feeling embarrassed at shoving food so quickly into his mouth, Red immediately wiped the crumbs from his mouth and hands.

She was almost the same height as Alexandros, with wavy chestnut-colored hair, and had the most appealing almond-shaped green eyes. He noticed she had something white pierced through her left ear. She wore a simple over the shoulder, tan, knee-length dress which could have easily once been a burlap bag, but on her, it was beautiful. He could not help but stare at this woman. There were only a few feet between them, but Red felt an overwhelming attraction, he felt as though he was being pulled towards her. He wanted to walk over to her and talk to her, but he knew that he could not.

Never before had Red thought of his inability to talk as a curse, but not being able to speak to this gorgeous creature was definitely a curse to him right now. Instead, he stood frozen in place, a thickness to the air made it hard for him to breathe.

Alexandros and the woman turned toward him now and chuckled good-heartedly as they walked over to where Red was standing.

"Nonie, this is Red. Red, this is Nonie. She lives here with Thug and Meme."

"Pozdrowienia," she said greeting Red.

She reached forward to touch Red's chest. Unsure of what she was about to do, Red stepped back.

"Easy lad, she wants to touch you. It is her greeting," Alexandros explained.

Nonie tried again. She reached out to touch Red's heart, and this time he did not move. She closed her eyes and tilted her head to the left. A look of calmness came over her. Her expression was that of softness and tenderness, revealing a sense of inner peace. As soon as Nonie touched Red, he felt warmth come from within. It seemed to radiate from Nonie's hand all the way through his chest and down to his toes. Red continued to stare at Nonie, his thoughts bursting with wonder.

Nonie opened her eyes, withdrew her hand and looked into Red's eyes. She said in a soft tone,

"czysty serce."

She smiled a loving warm smile as if the two had shared something special.

"Excuse me, but if you two are finished," Alexandros interjected, while looking at Red. "She said you have a pure heart." Looking away and heading toward the table again, Alexandros made an 'humph' sound. He turned and tore a chunk off of another roll and handed it to Nonie. Finally Red and Nonie broke eye contact, and with their faces a little flush, they turned to the large roll before them. Nonie began to nibble softly on the roll that was handed to her as Red mindlessly took another piece. Alexandros had two handfuls by now and was eating from both.

After the awkward silence, Red realized that Nonie had spoken in another language, yet Alexandros was able to understand her. Red looked to Alexandros. He pointed to his own lips and then to Alexandros. It was his way of asking how he understood Nonie.

"Oh you're wondering how I could understand her? Well that's easy. She speaks a form of Polchev, which is not too different from Gourmanese, a sister country to my homeland, Lanzeville." He explained as if Red should know of these places.

"Nonie was explaining to me before, that she is not a prisoner here, even though she spends her time in that habitat. She is free to move about as she wishes. It is for her safety, that she lives in there. You see the giants cannot see her when she is on the floor. It not only is her home right now, but Thug uses that cage to carry her around safely," explained Alexandros.

A look of understanding crossed his face and he felt a sense of relief that she was not a prisoner. Even though he had only just met Nonie, he did not like the thought of her being caged. Alexandros continued, "Her parents were killed and her sisters taken. She was alone and crying on the day Thug found her. He understood that she was alone, so he took her home so she would not be alone anymore." Alexandros took one last bite of the roll in his hand and put the remaining portion in his pocket. "One never knows when you will be locked away and need nourishment," he said.

Instantly, Red thought back to where he first met Alexandros, locked away in the Room of Need.

Alexandros could take one bread crumb and grow it into an entire loaf of bread. If he took all the crumbs and small objects out of his pocket and grew them to their full size, he could feed and furnish many villages for years to come.

"Dlaczego uzytkownik w tym miejscu?" asked Nonie, looking at Red and Alexandros.

"She would like to know why we are here," Alexandros translated to Red.

Alexandros explained to Nonie how they came to be with Thug, and how they brought him home by way of the Snar-bow. Nonie's eyes widened as if she were impressed.

"Dlaczego pomoc Thug?" She asked.

"We helped him, simply, because he needed it," he said in Polechev, defending his actions. Alexandros turned to Red, "She does not understand why we would want to help a stranger."

Chapter 12
Nonie

Once all three had finished their food, Thug came along and scooped them all up and placed them in Nonie's habitat.

"Sleep now," he said with a yawn.

The cage was much larger than it looked from the table. Once inside, Red looked around and noticed the beautifully-crafted furnishings. There was a wooden rocking chair that was so finely detailed, that Red felt he would defile it by sitting on it. The head- rest of the rocking chair had carvings of animals, some Red could identify, some he had never before seen. Each animal was so detailed that they looked like they could jump off of the woodwork. The spindles that supported the back were carved and shaped like intertwining roots from a tree, weaving in and out of each other. The rockers on the bottom had such an amazing design, that Red felt that this chair held the very heart of the forest. He knew that the maker of this rocking chair loved and respected the forest, as he did.

The bed that sat a few feet away was a masterpiece in its own design. Its frame looked as if it were spun from pure gold, thinned into strips, and then woven together. It was the most impressive bed Red had ever seen. Even the bedding was amazing and looked as if it were constructed from puffy white clouds. If you had ever looked up at the sky and imagined what it would be like to sleep on a cloud, this was it. Red and Alexandros looked around examining their surroundings with delicate care, neither wanted to miss a thing.

Finally, Alexandros spoke to Nonie, "ktorego tworzenie?"

Nonie pointed to herself and laughed finding the question amusing.

"She says she made this furniture," Alexandros said to Red in total awe and admiration. "It is the most intricate work I have ever seen. Never in my many years have I ever seen such exquisite detail." Alexandros moved closer to the bed, his fingers tracing the delicate weave.

"Uzytkownik podobnie jak?" She asked.

"Yes, yes of course we like it. It's amazing!" Alexandros said to Nonie. Turning to Red, he asked, "Can you believe she is surprised that we like it?"

With eyebrows raised and mouth open, Red looked at Nonie in stunned silence.

"I znaczeniu, co chce się."

"Very impressive," Alexandros said, and then translated to Red. "She just said that she can sense what the wood wants to be, and then makes it so."

Red wondered what else she was capable of making. He also wondered why she was surprised when they liked her wood carvings in her habitat. Red felt a sudden sadness for Nonie.

Once they had a good look around, Nonie invited them both to sit down.

Within minutes they all found a place to settle down to get some much needed rest. Red sat on the beautifully-crafted couch, while Alexandros made his way to the delicately- crafted dinner table and chairs. Alexandros pulled out a tiny stick from his robes and began cleaning his teeth. Nonie went to her bed and watched her new visitors until she fell asleep.

It felt like Red had only been asleep for a few minutes when all the commotion began. A loud, cracking noise filled the once silent air as the habitat shook violently. Quick as a blink, Alexandros's hand was on Red pulling him to the floor of the cage. Within minutes, everything changed. Suddenly, a once-beautiful and serene place to rest was now instantly a heap of twigs and broken boulders that nearly crushed their heads. Dazed and confused, Red looked around trying to make sense of what was happening. He felt pain shoot through his arm as he looked to Alexandros, who was gripping him fiercely. Red followed him quickly as they made their way out of the debris. Nonie was holding her head, as she ran. Red noticed blood rushing down her face and into her eyes. Alexandros grabbed her arm with his free hand and ran.

Boulders had been falling from the walls and the roof. Everywhere he looked rocks had tumbled out of their place. Red had thought earlier that the entire village looked unsteady, but what had caused the boulders to suddenly fall?

A sudden realization hit Red. While trying to run for safety, they would not be seen in the billowing clouds that lay at ground level. Red did not know where Thug and Meme were, but he hoped against hope that their feet did not suddenly appear over his head. Thug and Meme were not highly intelligent beings so he did not know how they would react in a crisis.

A very loud cry was heard off in the distance. Red needed to focus. He needed to concentrate on the layout of the giant's home to make it to the doorway. He tried to run in the direction of what he thought was the exit, but Alexandros tightened his already intense grip and pulled him in the opposite direction. Just then, Red heard a loud explosion and when he looked up, he saw an opening.

Sunlight was coming from the other side of the room and he also saw two little glowing lights, one pink and one blue. The colored lights shining through the falling boulders were that of Slo-zo and Tiddle-toa. Needing his hands to climb the pile of boulders that were now scattered over the floor, Alexandros let go of Red's arm, but still held firm to Nonie, who was having difficulty seeing through the blood that was still rushing down her face and eyes.

"Lad, run towards Slo-zo and Tiddle-toa. They will lead you to safety, go, go..." Alexandros yelled to Red.

Red continuously looked over his shoulder to his friends as he made his way out of the wreckage. Instead of continuing alone, Red decided he should help Alexandros guide Nonie over the heap of boulders that was once a house. Out of danger from falling boulders and in the open air, Red noticed all the structures that once housed giants were no more. All that remained were giants looking for their loved ones, calling out names with little or no response. Red felt a sadness for the giants. He wondered if they understood what had happened, especially since even he could hardly understand it, himself. At this moment, all Red knew for certain, was that the village had been destroyed by something unseen.

Smoke billowed from heaps of crushed rock, while the smell of burning wood filled Red's thoughts. It triggered a memory of his village, when the smell of wood was followed by fish cooking. Today, he did not like the smell of burning wood.

Slo-zo and Tiddle-toa led the party away from danger. It was very hard to see the direction in which they were heading. As long as it was away from danger, that was all that mattered. They ran as fast as they could, with the blue and pink Snars leading the way. When Red first met the Snars, he was amazed at their gorgeous colors but he did not remember seeing them glow. Like having a beacon showing you the way, they glowed brightly now.

"Look there, lad. We made it," Alexandros said, pointing to a cluster of Snars who were waiting for the fleeing group.

"Potrzebuję odpoczynku," Nonie added.

"We will rest when we know we are safe. Look there, the Snars are waiting to show us the way back. We will go to the ground below and find a place to camp," he said, between breaths.

Within a few minutes the group had made their way to the Snar-bow and was descending the stairs. Nonie had wiped away some of the blood from her eyes and was pushing it back, towards her hair. Her face looked as though she had washed with blood, instead of using soap and water. Even while she looked disheveled, Red thought she was the prettiest woman he had ever seen. With her long hair all matted, he thought that she looked like she had just fought a bear and won. She was a mess, yet so stunning. He wanted to give her a hug and tell her he would fight by her side any time. Instead, he descended the steps next to her. He reached up and put his hand on her shoulder and smiled, in an attempt to comfort her after the rush of excitement. It was his way of saying, 'I am here for you, and it will be ok.' He was not sure of just how everything would be okay. He just hoped it would be. In response, Nonie smiled a small smile. They continued down the stairs side by side with Alexandros in front of them with Slo-zo and Tiddle-toa taking the lead.

Once they reached the bottom and stepped away from the Snars, Red heard Alexandros whistle again. All the Snars responded to him at once, with a short sweet tune. Like a candle being snuffed, the Snars simultaneously stopped glowing, and were now back to their original vibrant colors. Just as they all came together to form the Snar-bow, they all broke apart with an explosion of color, very similar to fireworks with color flying off in every direction, to once again become part of the everyday scenery. It was a very impressive sight. Red knew he would never forget these amazing creatures. He smiled and waved as they disbursed, forever grateful for their help.

Chapter 13
Ludlow

The party walked until they entered an area where the trees were thickly settled but still sparse enough for the group to make camp.

Once everyone had a chance to catch their breath, they listened intently, as Nonie questioned Alexandros.

"Do you think Meme and Thug will be okay? Nothing like that had ever happened since I had lived there," Nonie asked, in her native language.

"Good question, lass, but I am not sure I can answer that one with certainty. However, I do know that they are a strong family. Hopefully, Thug and Meme will be okay, and able to rebuild their homes. Even more astonishing, is that *we* made it out of there alive. If not for the Snars, we might not have survived. I am truly thankful for their service,."

Nonie continued in Polechev, "what happened? What caused the land to shake up where there is no real land?"

"Ahh, lass what caused that, indeed? That is exactly the right question," Alexandros added, as he walked around in lazy circles, contemplating the answer.

Alexandros walked over to a knee-high boulder and sat down. "I can summon a familiar and have them go check on Thug and Meme, if that will set your mind at ease," he suggested.

"Would you?" She asked, sounding hopeful and excited. "They have been my family since mine was..... I mean since, I came to live with them," Nonie replied in her native language.

Exasperated, Red threw his hands in the air feeling frustrated and left out of the conversation. *What are you saying*! He yelled with his inner monologue, since he is the only one in the group that does not speak or understand Polechev.

Alexandros noticed Red's hands in the air and said, "I am sorry lad. The two of you, should be able to communicate with each other." He walked over to Nonie, squatted down next to her, and reached for the white bone in her ear. Without removing it, he put the palm of his right hand over her ear. The air between her ear and Alexandros's hand began to dance and sway, like smoke rising from a fire. A minute later, black lines appeared and began to swirl around the bone, moving this way and that. Red noticed that Alexandros's eyes were fixed on him. He did not know exactly what was going on, and Red was more than curious as to why Alexandros was eyeing him. Once the lines on the bone stopped moving, Alexandros withdrew his palm, stood up and stepped away.

"Go on then, try it," he said to Nonie.

"Try what?" Nonie replied obviously confused.

Red's eyes went wide as he understood her. For the first time since they met, Red understood the words she spoke.

"That's a good lass. Now, where is that water? I know it's here. I can hear it," he said, as he walked off between the trees.

Turning to Red, Nonie said, "Can you hear me? I know you hear me, I mean, but can you really understand me?" she asked excitedly.

He nodded and smiled enthusiastically. It was amazing to both Nonie and Red that they no longer needed a translator. Nonie touched the bone in her ear. It now had pure magic flowing through it.

"I am glad he did not alter it too much. I don't want anything to happen to it. It has sentimental value." Without being prompted for an explanation, she began to tell her story.

On a cool spring day, when I was a young girl, I was on a day trip with my mother, father, and three sisters. We had just settled down to have a picnic when suddenly we were attacked. The creatures were none that I had ever seen before, or since. They looked to be ordinary men, with one exception; they had large bird wings extending from their shoulder blades.

My mother and father were killed almost instantly trying to defend their children. My sisters and I ran to hide behind the trees. Shedoe, my oldest sister, was the first to be taken by the attackers.

Next to be taken was Hyori, she's my second oldest sister. When I stepped away from the tree with my youngest sister Haslena, we threw whatever size rocks we could find. One fist-size rock made contact with a birdman's shoulder as he was trying to fly away with Hyori. He turned suddenly, dropped Hyori to the ground and charged for me instead. I grabbed the closest stick and swung it as he dove in for the attack. I heard a loud crack as the stick made contact and broke his arm. The skin tore open and a piece of the wood was now embedded in his arm. As he tore the wood out, a sliver of bone came out with it. With intense pain shooting through his arm, he chose to retreat. He began to fly away sweeping down towards Haslena. Using his only working arm, he grabbed her by her hair and flew away. I ran towards my remaining sister, Hyori. Before I could get to her, the last birdman appeared out of nowhere and took her too. I was left there alone, holding nothing but the bone fragment that the birdman had thrown to the ground. Then without warning, and before any birdmen came back for me, I appeared to be in different place after what I thought was only a few steps. Next thing I knew, I was in a land of giants. That is where I met Thug.

As a reminder of my great loss, I took the bone and pierced it through my ear, and swore to avenge my stolen family.

Red listened to her tale. He felt an overwhelming sadness for her. He reached out and held her hand, comforting her as she cried. Red hoped that in time, Nonie could see that Alexandros had turned something that was so tragic into something good and useful. Red's heart ached for her. He wished he could erase such a tragedy from her life.

He released Nonie's hand quickly and stood as he saw that Alexandros was carrying a large leaf, filled with water. As he walked, droplets splashed over the side.

Nonie took a step forward, "where did you find a tree with such huge leaves?" she asked, while quickly wiping away her tears.

"A wizard uses what he must," he said as he looked from Nonie to Red. He obviously noticed her puffy, moist eyes, but did not ask why she had been crying.

Red knew the truth to Alexandros's words. He had seen Alexandros make tiny objects into larger ones. Just recently he had made a piece of wood the size of a toothpick increase to the size of a staff, which he used to defend them against the purple ladybugs. Red assumed that Alexandros had taken a regular size leaf and made it grow to suit his needs, thus creating a wash basin.

"Here you go, lass. Ladies, first." Alexandros gestured toward the water. Nonie went to the water and began to wash. When she had finished cleaning the blood from her face and hair, Alexandros went to her and examined her wounds. "You have a deep laceration on your temple. Remain still."

Nonie did as she was instructed, while Alexandros held his hands over her head. Red watched as Nonie's wound began to shimmer and magically heal. Within a few seconds her wound was gone completely. Nonie reached up and felt her head, "thank you," she said with a smile.

"My pleasure," Alexandros replied, tenderly. Not finished working his magic, he went to the water basin and stuck an index finger into the water. When he withdrew it, the tip of his finger was covered in dirt and blood. Without a second thought, Alexandros flicked his finger and thumb. The dirt and blood on the tip of his finger magically disappeared. Red smiled in amazement. *Incredible,* he thought as he took his turn washing. When Red was finished with the water, Alexandros again stuck his finger into it and flicked away the dirt. Finally, it was Alexandros's turn to wash, and when he finished he touched the giant leaf with his open hand, but this time the leaf collapsed and the water spilled to the ground.

"Now that we are clean and rested, let us discuss our travel plans, shall we?" Alexandros said.

"Oh, umm, I don't really have any," Nonie replied.

"Well, I am assisting Red to his village, I think. If I am not mistaken, he is somewhat lost. After that, I will return to my home in Lanzeville. If you would like to travel with us, we would love to have you," he said.

"Well, if you do not mind a tag-a-long, I would like that very much," she said, as she looked to Red for his approval. Which of course, he nodded his agreement.

"Well, lass, that makes it unanimous," said Alexandros, as he sat down on a knee- high rock.

"For the Love of Merlin!" Alexandros exclaimed, as he jumped up quickly.

Red was startled when Alexandros suddenly called out. He looked at the source of the excitement. He noticed a head and neck appearing out from where Alexandros had just sat down. What looked like a rock, now turned out to be something that swayed and trembled. As it shook off the dirt, it revealed a shell.

"Ludlow? Ludlow, Is that you?" Alexandros exclaimed.

"Sir, is that you? Could it be?" Ludlow asked with a yawn.

"What are you doing here, and... why are you a giant snail?" Alexandros asked.

"Well, sir, I have been in this form since the morning you left. It is the last spell you taught me, remember? I wanted to demonstrate to you that I had mastered that transformation spell. But, on the morning you disappeared, I was the one who was surprised, because I could not shape back since you had not taught me that yet," replied Ludlow.

"Ludlow, I hope you know that I left on a sudden quest to help a woman in need. I did not intentionally desert you. I was actually held captive all these years. It was not until a few days ago, that I was released," Alexandros explained.

"No... Tell me that is not true. Who? Who held you?" Ludlow asked, incredulously.

"First, let me apologize to you for your predicament. It is due to my capture that you have been forced to remain as an oversized snail. For that I am truly sorry, Ludlow." Alexandros knelt down and hugged his old friend. "It does me well to see you. Let me introduce you to my friends." he said as he stood. "This beautiful lass, is Nonie. She has been a resident of the giant land as of late. This strapping, young lad is Red. He is from a far-away land, and he holds his tongue as you hold your valor."

Nonie bowed as she was introduced, and Red nodded and waved his greetings.

How incredible it must be to live one's life as a wizard, Red thought.

"It is my esteemed pleasure to make your acquaintance," Ludlow said to them both.

"Would you allow me to help you shape out, Ludlow?" asked Alexandros.

"Well, sir, if it will not displease you, I would very much like to remain as I am. I have been this way for so long, that I am afraid of what my wife and children would do if they saw me in human form. It would certainly make family time a bit awkward," he said as he chuckled.

"Oh, Ludlow, it really does me good to see you," Alexandros laughed.

"Sir, you must not make me wait much longer. You must tell me how and why you were captured, or my shell might burst with anticipation," Ludlow said.

"Ludlow, you always did want to get right down to business. I remember how you would always read the end of my journals, first expecting a secret to reveal itself to you. Do you remember?" Alexandros asked.

"Yes, sir, I do," replied Ludlow. "Do you remember the time you cursed the book, *A Wizards guide to mushroom making*? That little trick turned my fingers into mushrooms, and it took me weeks to learn how to transfigure them back."

Red and Nonie all laughed at Ludlow's misadventures with the wizard. Red had only known Alexandros for a few days, and already he had heard at least a dozen stories.

Chapter 14
Change of plans

As Alexandros and Ludlow reconnected and shared more stories, Red and Nonie made a campfire and listened to the two friends talk and laugh.

After a while, the laughter ended and Alexandros began to tell Ludlow how he ended up in The Room of Need. Everyone was so silent that the only sound Red could hear was the rapid beating of his own heart. He felt a wave of sadness for Alexandros. *Who would lock away such a wondrous man?*

"It was fate that brought this young lad to my door," Alexandros said, waving a hand toward Red. And fate is not finished with us yet," he said.

"A wise man once said to me, 'if man was meant to look backward, he would have had eyes on the back of his head'," Ludlow said encouragingly.

"What does that mean?" Nonie asked sounding confused.

"Well, lass, Alexandros explained, it's a way of expressing that you should live for today, and not dwell on your past."

"I see, but, isn't sharing stories from your past a way of looking backward too?" She asked.

"It is all fine and good to share stories amongst friends, but to live in the past and not let it go, well that could prevent you from developing a strong and healthy future," Alexandros replied tenderly.

Red nodded his agreement, while his thoughts drifted to his home. For a moment, he could not concentrate on the here and now. He wondered if he should be doing more to get back home or if he too was just living in the past. His attention was brought back to the present when Ludlow spoke again.

Ludlow began to tell more stories that held their attention throughout the rest of the night. He told the story of how he met his wife, Gladys, and of their numerous children. He went on to tell of his emptiness without his mentor and how his need to find him had grown stronger every day, as if a piece of him were missing. Ludlow explained that he had felt a sense of disconnect. So he had started his search for Alexandros.

"Ludlow, you took time away from your family to find me?" Alexandros asked incredulously.

"Sir, you would have done the same for me. There is so much I must tell you of Lanzeville. So much has happened since your departure. First, Ovarb is gone. He was killed during a routine training exercise. He should never have been part of the training exercise.

Supposedly, at the last minute, the Captain of the Guards became ill and Ovarb took his place," Ludlow explained.

"Who is Ovarb?" Nonie asked.

"My brother, the greatest King Lanzeville has ever known," Alexandros said sadly.

"I am sorry for your loss," Nonie said to Alexandros.

Red gave a sympathetic smile.

"Thank you, Lass." Turning to Ludlow he asked, "Who is King now?"

"Before I reveal who is King, let me tell you what has happened since your absence," Ludlow said.

"The King has given his army the power to carry out swift punishment. They are allowed to kill a man for the slightest of infractions. If you are caught stealing or hoarding, you may be executed. There is no trial or punishment. There is only final judgment," Ludlow said, with his head low at the thought of those who had been killed, unjustly.

"That is no way to live. How do you defend yourself if wrongly accused?" Nonie pleaded.

"Exactly, Madame, you cannot. You are given final judgment as a way to teach others and keep order," Ludlow explained.

"You still have yet to tell me who the King is," Alexandros pleaded.

"Sir, you already know the answer. Deep inside, you wanted to believe he was good. You had always wanted him to be a good man. We have known since his birth he was not fit to wear the crown. He has always taken what he thought was his to take. He murdered his own father, your brother, and has made it look like an accident," Ludlow said, sourly.

"Edic," Alexandros said softly.

"Yes sir. Edic, your nephew, is now the King," Ludlow repeated, as confirmation.

"How far is Lanzeville from where we sit now, Ludlow?"

"Well sir, I estimate it to be three days travel, if we were all snails. But, for those of you with legs, it would only be a matter of hours, due north," Ludlow said, trying to make light of the heavy subject.

"For the Love of Merlin!" Alexandros shouted again, as he leapt up in surprise. "I am almost home and I did not even know it? The scenery has changed so much. I might have kept going on had we not run into you, Ludlow. Again, fate has stepped in to show us the way."

"Sir, you have been gone many years. I fear you would not even recognize Lanzeville had you lived here all these years. Edic has made many changes. He tore down Ovarb's castle and reconstructed one in his own honor. He has enslaved and taxed his townsmen so much that they all welcome death as a relief from servitude." Ludlow shook his head side to side, in sympathy for his fellow townsmen. When he spoke next, he lifted his head high and proud, "even though I have been in this form for many years, I have had a very fortunate life. I am slave to no King. I serve only my wife and family. That is why I wish to remain as I am."

Alexandros knelt down in front of Ludlow and boasted,

"My dear friend, I dare not transform you. You are a better man than I ever hoped you would be. You are a loyal and dear friend. Come morning we shall return to Lanzeville. That is, if Red and Nonie do not mind a slight change in plans. I do promise to help you find your way, lad. A wizard never forgets a promise. And speaking of promises, I have another to attend too, as he swirled his hand in the air. Three birds appeared out of nowhere and landed on his shoulder. They bounced and chirped excitedly.

"Go to the land of the giants and see if they are okay," Alexandros asked of his feathered familiars. The birds flew off his shoulder and flew up and out of sight flapping their colorful wings. "Now then, you two get some sleep while we go for a walk," Alexandros suggested, as he and Ludlow walked toward the trees.

When morning came and Red awoke, he noticed the same three birds from last night on Alexandros's shoulder again. They chirped and danced in place. Alexandros thanked them,, as they flew away. Red sat up and brushed the dirt from his face and hair.

"Ah, morning, lad. My little ones reported that all is well in the land of the giants. They are rebuilding their homes and are already half finished. Still no word as to why it happened. One of life's little mysteries that we may never understand," Alexandros said.

Red glanced around looking for Nonie. She was not laying down where she had fallen asleep last night. Alexandros spoke up, "Do not worry my friend, she is doing her lady business over there." He pointed at a cluster of bushes next to two large trees. Red watched as the bushes moved slightly then he quickly looked away to give Nonie some privacy. Since she was now out of sight, Red thought it would be a good time to make himself a bit more presentable. He began to bang the dirt off of the animal skin that he wore until the cloud of dust surrounding him dissipated. Next, he used his open fingers like a comb and ran them through his hair repeatedly until the tangles were gone.

"If you wish to have a bath there is a spring fifty paces east. Ludlow and I happened upon it last night during our walk," Alexandros offered while turning around and pointing towards a small break between the trees. Red decided he would take advantage of the spring and go take a bath.

As Alexandros had said, the spring was fifty paces away. Red removed his animal skin and soaked himself in the spring until he felt clean. His hair had been sticking to his head while the dirt flowed down his face. It seemed that his hair had grown a considerable length since leaving his village. Red wondered briefly about his return to his village. Would he look older? He already felt older and no longer the innocent boy of fifteen. He felt more mature. He started to think about what his mother had said in the brief time they had together.

"When you awake, you will no longer be in the Bonk Bonk village. You will no longer be my son. You will leave all your family behind, until you can find your way home. If you can find your way back to the elders, then you will be a man. You, my son, will have proven you belong to the Bonk Bonk tribe. Go forth and fear not. Use your head and choose your words wisely, for they have more power than you know. Take with you the knowledge that the Spirits are there for you when you need it."

It was starting to make sense to him now, when she said "you will no longer be my son," she was not disowning him. It was her way of telling him that he needed to leave his emotions and connections to the tribe behind him, and focus on the task before him. She had also said he would return a man. Did she know it would take a long time to return, or did she mean that he would mature so much that he would feel like a man, like the way he was feeling right now? Red wondered why he had been chosen to leave the village. None of his siblings were sent away. *Why me? Did I do something wrong? Why couldn't I have been given the "Hunt", as my test. Oh, yeah, because I was a failure at hunting.*

Red looked up quickly when he noticed Nonie walking into the clearing. He was thankful that he had just finished putting on his animal skin. He smiled a greeting as he tried to look casual leaning against a tree.

"Sorry. Did I startle you?" She asked. Red shook his head. "Can I talk to you for a minute? I didn't want to alarm Alexandros and Ludlow, but I can sense a lot of trouble ahead. I know that if we find Edic someone will die." Red's eyes went wide in surprise. He tilted his head slightly to the side, concentrating on what Nonie had just said.

Before he knew it Nonie was standing before him with her wavy hair in her face. *She is absolutely breathtaking,* he thought. Nonie smiled at him and kissed his cheek.

"Thank you, you really think so?" She asked. Red's eyes went wide, *I didn't speak. I was thinking it. Can you read my mind?* He asked in thought.

"I can read yours," she replied with a playful, grin. "Don't change the subject. Did you hear me? I said, if we go after Edic, someone will die," She warned.

Yes, I heard you. How long have you been able to read my mind? He asked again with only his thoughts.

"When I was a young girl I had many talents, and surprisingly, since this very morning, some have returned."

Whoa, he thought.

"And for the record, you're pretty breath-taking, yourself," she said, blushing.

Thank you. But, let's get back to the seriousness of death. Do you know who will die? He tried to keep his mind on the subject. He tried to stay focused. Looking into her gorgeous eyes made it hard for him to concentrate.

"Well, I see a lot of darkness around Alexandros. But, that does not mean it is him. It could be that someone close to him will die, and that is why I am sensing it. It would be horrible if it were Ludlow. Those two really care for each other and they have just reunited. It would be such a tragedy," Nonie said, sadly.

We must help Alexandros in any way we can without any of us dying, of course.

"You know, you are a good man, Red. You are everything Shelu wanted you to be. She is very proud of you."

Red stood frozen in his tracks. When he was able to move he grabbed Nonie by the shoulders. He looked deeply into her eyes and projected his thoughts. *How do you know of my mother? How do you know her name?*

Chapter 15
Lanzeville

He could not believe his ears. Why would Nonie mention his mother and how does she know her name? He felt a pain in his chest from Nonie's sharp words. They pierced his heart and held him in place. When he was able to compose himself, he asked her again, *"How do you know my mother?"*

"I told you, I have many special gifts. Not only can I hear your thoughts but I can also speak to spirits. Now please let me go, your starting to hurt me."

I am sorry. I did not mean to hurt you. Are you saying my mother speaks to you from the spirit world? he thought as he released his grip.

"I know a lot about you. For instance, I know why you are unable to speak. Long ago, your village was cursed and put under a spell. Since then no one ever speaks. You have the ability, but with consequences." While Nonie spoke, Red noticed tears swelling in her eyes.

Why are you crying? He asked.

"I can feel the pain it has caused you. I feel the sadness in your heart from when your mother died, the night you were born. Not only can I hear your thoughts but I feel your pain, and your sadness. I don't know why, but, ever since I met you, many of my dormant gifts have...awakened."

I am sorry, Nonie. I do not want you to know my pain. It is not your burden to carry. Is there anything I can do?

"Yes, let go of your pain and live for today. Just as Alexandros always says...Do not live in the past. You will return home when it is time. For now, do not worry for Shelu or your village. Both are well."

So far you have told me that my thoughts and feelings cause you pain. My mother's spirit talks to you, and someone is going to die. Is there anything else? He thought.

"Nope, that's it," She replied. She turned on her heels and started back to camp. He noticed the smile Nonie had given him before turning and heading back. Red could not shake the feeling that there was more information Nonie was not sharing with him. He wished she could not hear his thoughts. He knew that his feelings for her were growing and he would not be able to hide them any longer. She probably already suspected, since she was most likely listening to him right now.

"I am, and I love you too," She yelled over her shoulder to him.

Mud Pies! Red exclaimed in thought. He had just realized he needed to learn how to keep his thoughts focused. But, when it came to Nonie, he could not help himself. Right now he needed to really work on shifting his focus and thoughts to Alexandros. He wanted to be able to help him in any way he could. He was unsure what they would face in Lanzeville, but the one thing he did know, was that he was willing to fight to the death, for the safety of his friends.

Red and Nonie entered the camp while Alexandros was snuffing the fire out with a burst of magic from his fingertips. For a wizard, it was just as easy as blowing out a candle with your breath.

"Time to go," Alexandros said.

"Stay close. We do not want either of you to fall victim to Final Judgment," Ludlow warned.

All three followed Ludlow as he lead the party out of camp and enroute to Lanzeville. You might think that a snail leading the way would be slow going, but he was a large snail, so, amazingly, it was a good pace.

They walked for a long time before anyone spoke. It was Ludlow who broke the silence first.

"Over the next hill, will be the first of the outer villages to Lanzeville."

"Are you okay, Alexandros?" Nonie asked.

"Oh lass, it is not I that you should be worried about," Alexandros replied, and Ludlow began to chuckle as he thought about Edic getting what he really deserves.

"The people are scared of Edic, and may not come out of their homes. The less we interact with them the safer it will be for all," Ludlow reminded the group.

They entered the small village and right away Red noticed the emptiness. There was one man on horseback patrolling the only street that lead in and out of town. He was dressed in a blue uniform with "Edicton Guard" in red letters, on the back of his tunic. It left no question as to whom who he worked for.

"Edic-ton," Nonie stressed the word as if it were poison.

"Well, that's new," Alexandros said with obvious distaste.

As they walked slowly into town the group noticed the houses were closed tight; not a window or door left had been left open to let in the light. No animals were seen, no pigs in their pens, no dogs barking, and no cats lying lazily in the sun. It was as if the Edicton Guard occupied the entire town alone.

Ludlow broke the eerie silence, "As I remember, this town had the best baker. People would line up before he opened his door to buy his fresh bread."

"Where are the people now?" Nonie whispered.

"They are here, in their homes. They are too afraid to break any of Edic's laws, so they stay indoors as much as possible," Ludlow replied.

"Let us move swiftly," Alexandros encouraged.

The patrolling horseman eyed the group suspiciously as they entered town. When the travelers did nothing to cause any enforcement of Final Judgment, he let them go without a word. Once the group had exited the town, they all exhaled a collective sigh of relief.

"One down, three to go," Ludlow stated as he led the way through the remaining three towns. Each visit ended with similar results. Each town's guard had a spin-off of Edic's name on their tunics: Edicville, Edicson, and finally Edicterstonville.

Once they reached the road to Lanzeville, Nonie spoke freely:

"Well, he obviously saved the best name for last," she said with a giggle.

"It appears he is not very creative," Ludlow added.

"So it seems," Alexandros agreed as they continued down the road until Nonie suddenly stopped.

"Did you hear that?" Nonie asked.

"What, dear, what did you hear?" Alexandros asked.

"Shh, there it is again." Nonie held her hand up to halt the group.

What are you hearing? Red thought.

"Shh."

"No one spoke, lass, who are you shh-ing?" Alexandros asked.

"I can hear them. I can hear my sisters. Oh, dear spirits, they are not of this world." That was all she said before she collapsed to the ground.

Chapter 16
Strength in numbers

It took some time before Nonie could stop crying. Every time she tried to compose herself, she would start to cry all over again.

"I have been without my sisters for many years, but, I never thought of them as entering the spirit world."

It's okay Nonie, thought Red.

"I know, but it still hurts," Nonie said, holding back tears.

"What exactly did you hear, lass?" Alexandros asked.

"Well, I thought I heard Hyori, one of my older sisters, say, 'May the spirits guide you'."

"Are you sure it was Hyori?" Ludlow asked.

"Yes! I was much younger when I last saw her. But, I know my sister's voice. I did not say anything earlier to either of you, but I can hear the spirit world. I am sorry for not saying anything sooner."

"Lass, do not ever apologize for keeping your gifts to yourself. They are for you to share with whomever you choose," replied Alexandros soothingly, as he tenderly placed a hand on her shoulder.

"Well, until recently, some of my gifts were dormant, but ever since I woke up this morning, I have been able to hear thoughts."

"So, your saying you can talk to the spirit world, and read minds?" Alexandros asked.

"I cannot read your thoughts or Ludlow's, but so far just his," she said pointing to Red, who flashed a sheepish grin.

Ludlow started pacing, or rather gliding back and forth. "I wonder," he said curiously.

"What?" Nonie responded, as Red helped her to her feet.

"Let us assume for a moment your sisters have passed. Hyori said, 'May the spirits guide you'. But, if she were actually a spirit, would she not then say, "I am here with you", or, "we will guide you"," Ludlow said.

"What do you mean?' Nonie asked.

"It's just that I find it curious."

"You are *too* curious, my apprentice. Come, let us keep moving." Alexandros instructed, ending the conversation and resuming the trek home.

As they walked, the road curved to the right. Once they reached the bend, Red could see a prominent incline in the road. At the end of the road, the entrance to Lanzeville could be seen. A large sign was posted on double stone pillars declaring its name. The intensity in the air could be felt all around. Alexandros inhaled deeply and said, "Here we go."

Lanzeville was much different than the surrounding villages. Here, the people were out and about, conducting their daily chores. There were women hanging laundry, men chopping wood, and customers in the bakery. Red noticed guards patrolling on horseback just as he had seen in the other villages. The only difference was the gold lettering on these tunics instead of the red.

Alexandros still witnessed the proof of Edic's rule. The people appeared to be laboring about their lives as if they were not being threatened on a daily basis, yet it still looked like he was watching a morbid play where each actor is acting out their parts with fear in their eyes. One wrong word or action could be their last.

They continued up the road until they were within a hundred paces from the castle gates. Just then, two of the guards stopped patrolling. They looked at the travelers, and then suddenly tore off their tunics to reveal their massive wings.

The two guards simultaneously extended their wings and attacked the stunned group. One birdman took hold of Nonie by her shoulders and took flight. The other guard attacked Alexandros and Ludlow, both instantly creating a tornado of dirt that began circling the lunging birdman. His attempt to attack first, had failed. The experienced wizards were quicker. Instantly, the single birdman was held captive as the tornado of dirt began to form a solid cocoon around his body. With his arms, legs, and wings pinned to him, leaving only his head exposed. Alexandros and Ludlow stepped in closer.

The attack was over so quickly that Red couldn't believe it. It was all finished within a matter of seconds. He looked around in a panic and could not see Nonie anywhere. Red had seen the birdman take Nonie and fly away. He was unsure where or why she was taken. One thing was for sure, he would do anything to find her. He stilled looked but there was no sign of her in any of the treetops, nor could he see her clinging to the castle walls. Red had no idea how to find her and he could feel his stomach turn as he felt alone in the world, again.

Just then Red remembered Nonie was able to read his thoughts. He projected his thoughts and called to her, *I will find you*!

It was not long after, that he heard a loud thunderous crack, shaking him out of his concentration. He looked over to the source of the sound and noticed the dirt cocoon was getting tighter and tighter. From the look in the birdman's eyes, it was clear that he was having difficulty breathing. His eyes were bulging and his face was turning red.

"You will tell us what we want to know, or you will never fly the friendly skies again," threatened Alexandros, as he closed in on the birdman.

"First things, first. Tell us who you are and why Nonie was taken," Ludlow inquired.

"That is none of your concern," he spat.

"It would be a pity to have an unmarked grave at the castle gates," Alexandros replied coldly.

"That's right", Ludlow joined in quickly.

"Refuse to talk, birdman and I will make it so you never speak again. Do not take my appearance for lack of ability." Red knew that Ludlow wanted to unleash his powers on the birdman. He could hear the anticipation in his voice.

Although they were attempting to find out who took Nonie, and for what purpose, it was not quick enough. Red felt as though he needed to take action. He walked up to their captive and punched him in the face, blood instantly gushing down his nose. The birdman, unable to do anything about it, turned his head away. Even with a broken nose he refused to talk.

"Red, calm yourself. We will find her," Alexandros said, turning his attention back to their prisoner. Red stepped away as the inquiry continued.

"You can either tell us why you took the girl, or we will let the villagers have you. I am sure they have years of pent up anger that they would like to let go of. Make your decision, us, or them!" he said as a crowd was now forming at the foot of the hill.

"You will never find her. When we take someone, they never return," he said after he spat out the blood that was dripping into his mouth.

"Tell me why you took her! This is your last chance," Alexandros said. He began to circle his hands over each other and they started to glow red and orange. It looked like he was creating fire in his palms.

"I will tell you nothing!"

"I suggest you make peace with your maker. You will be seeing him soon," Alexandros said. The birdman flinched as much as he could, thinking the fire ball was meant for him. With a flick of his wrist Alexandros sent the ball of flame into the air above the village. Once it exploded, a rush of people came out of their homes and shops to see what was happening. Alexandros addressed the unsettled crowd.

"I am Alexandros, brother to your fallen King Ovarb. These men have terrorized you for far too long. My friends and I are going to put an end to your oppression. Do what you wish to this creature, but help us. Someone here must know a way into the castle, besides the obvious front gates." The crowd stood quiet. No one moved, for fear had made them submissive over the years.

"I know a way," said a ten-year-old boy stepping through the crowd.

"What is your name, lad?" Alexandros asked.

"They call me, Mouse," he said.

"Thank you, Mouse. You know a way into the castle?" Ludlow asked, in confirmation.

"Yes. My job is Messenger for the cook. She sends me all over and I have to be quick about it. I can get you into the castle quicker than anyone here could," Mouse said boastfully.

"Then make haste, lad, Alexandros directed, "Show us the way."

"Follow me!" Mouse said, as he led them along the castle wall and away from the gates.

It only took minutes, before Red could hear screams coming from the birdman, who had been left with the villagers. Then just as quickly as he heard the screams begin, they ended. Red had not experienced first-hand, the villagers' way of life, but he was sure they took pleasure in their justice.

Chapter 17
Quiet as a Mouse

It did not take long for Mouse to lead them to a hidden passage. It looked like a boulder had been removed to create an entrance in the castle wall.

"This will take us to the kitchen or deeper into the castle, depending on where you want to go," Mouse explained.

"We need to find our friend that was taken from us, not find a bite to eat...take us deeper and let's hurry," Alexandros.

"Ok, stay close to me, it's dark in here," Mouse warned. He then led the way toward the bowels of the castle.

Once they had all crossed the threshold that brought them into the darkness, the group simultaneously grabbed hold of the person in front of them. Mouse was in the lead, next was Alexandros, holding the boy's tunic, and then Red followed Alexandros, with a handful of the wizards' robes. Bringing up the rear was Ludlow with his excellent night vision.

"I travel these passageways every day. I know every twist and turn. Sometimes, the cook throws me out of the kitchen for any reason she can think of. Of course, she doesn't know that I keep food hidden here. I put bread and apples in a sack and place a bucket over it. Then I cover it with rocks, so that the rats don't eat it. You won't tell, will you?" Mouse sounded regretful of his confession.

"You are a clever lad. We will not say a word," promised Alexandros, quietly to the young man. You did not need to see Mouse's face to know that the compliment made him smile.

The group continued through musty passageways, where darkness overruled the light that peeked through the cracks in the mortar. Soon they came to a round hole in the ceiling, where the air smelled horrid with the stench of rotten food. Red's feet felt the soft mush at the same moment his nose sensed the offending odor. He assumed food was discarded down the hole that he was standing in, instead of respectfully being thrown into a barrel. Since their eyes had already adjusted to the total darkness, the light making its way from the kitchen was a strain on their eyes.

"Up there, is the kitchen. Don't let the cook see you. She will punish me, if she sees us."

"Why do you keep wanting to go to the kitchen? Lead us down into the the dungeon, Mouse. We need to find our friend, Nonie," Alexandros pleaded.

"I don't think she will be in the dungeon. Only villagers who have broken the laws get put in the dungeon. If King Edic took her for himself, she will be with the others, and that means we have to pass by the kitchen." Mouse answered, confidently.

"What others? What do you mean?" asked Ludlow.

"Well, I know that the king has a room where he keeps "special" prisoners. I realized this because once, when I was exploring the castle, I crawled through some tunnels and I saw some women in cages, who looked clean and fed. One woman was in a cage alone and the other women were in the other cage, together. They were all beautiful women, yet they looked similar, like maybe they were sisters or something. I am thinking that one of them might be your friend," Mouse explained.

Red knew instantly that Mouse meant Nonie and her sisters. Nonie had shared with Red that her sisters were taken away by birdmen. It must be the same birdmen that are working for the king. *What does Edic want with Nonie and her sister's?* Red wondered.

"Interesting," Alexandros muttered quizzically, stroking his enormously long beard.

"We have to take the servant stairs from this point. If anyone asks what we are doing, let me do the talking," Mouse said. He continued on until they came to a wall. At that point, Mouse pushed a stone forward, until it was out of the way. From there, everyone had to climb out of the hidden passageway and onto the open staircase.

Once everyone had stepped clear, Mouse replaced the stone to hide his secrets once more. "Up there,"

Mouse instructed and pointed the way. So, up the stairs they went. Red had never seen so many steps in all his life. He thought back to the Bonk Bonk village, where he was accustomed to climbing steep hills, and some of those hills had crude steps carved into them, making the climb easier. Today, however, Red climbed so many steps, that he felt as if he would never lift his legs again.

"There are 2,012 steps from the kitchen to the forbidden wing. I counted them all," Mouse announced proudly.

"What are you doing here you filthy rat? You know you are not allowed here. Now get back to the kitchen you disgusting bag of bones!" screamed an old woman who was suddenly coming down the stairs.

"I am on King Edic's orders to...."

"How dare you speak to me. You are never to speak to me!" Without warning, she smacked Mouse across the face with such force that he was thrown backwards right off his feet and down a flight of stairs. Obviously not satisfied with such minor punishment, she raised her hand again as she descended the stairs to hit him once more. When she began to step past Alexandros, he stepped in front her.

"Madam, if you hit that boy again you will live the rest of your days wishing you had not."

"This is none of your business, you vile, old man!" she spat out, as she pushed Alexandros aside. Seizing the moment when the old woman put her hands on him,

Alexandros cast a spell that instantly turned the woman into what she had hated most, a filthy rat.

"Whoa," said Mouse. He was now standing and hiding behind Red.

"Are you okay, Mouse?" asked Alexandros.

"Yeah, I am great! I can't believe you did that for me!" he said, in amazement.

"No one should be treated in such a despicable way," the wizard replied.

"You were too lenient, Sir. If that were me, I would have turned her into a slimy wart-filled toad," added Ludlow.

Red smiled and watched the rat scurry down the stairs. Then from out of nowhere a cat appeared and chased the rat down into the depths of the castle. Alexandros glared at Ludlow, feigning disapproval.

"Ludlow, was that necessary?"

"What? I thought she could use a little exercise. She was a bit round in the middle," replied Ludlow. They all began to laugh, forgetting that they were supposed to be quiet. Before the laughter had a chance to die there was a sudden thump on the landing as a birdman appeared.

Ludlow not wanting to miss the chance to flex his abilities, turned the birdman into a bird, no longer a hybrid. Now unable to fight the intruders, the bird fluttered its wings and flew around in a panic. Alexandros ascended the stairs and grabbed the bird with one hand. With his other hand, he closed it tight around the bird, covering it. When he opened his hands again the bird was gone. One single feather fell from his fingertips to the floor.

"Good one, Sir," Ludlow said, approvingly.

"Let us make haste and find our friend," Alexandros replied with a smile. Red nodded his head in agreement. He wanted to get Nonie back soon.

At the top of the stairs, they turned right and onward, to the only door in the hall. It was a large wooden door with a round brass knocker. Mouse reached for the knocker to pull the door open. Without warning, the entire door crumbled to dust. The brass knocker crashed to the floor with a loud clang. Alexandros and Ludlow quickly looked to each other, to see who was responsible. Alexandros shrugged his shoulders and Ludlow shook his head side to side. *If neither of them was responsible for the door crumbling to dust, then who was?* Red thought.

Sensing danger ahead, in less time than it takes to blink Alexandros instinctively reached over to Mouse and grabbed his shoulder, pulled him close and quickly mumbled a spell. With his free hand, Alexandros gave a quick tap of his hand on the boy's head, and Mouse was gone from sight.

Three startled birdmen, inside the room, sprang into action. Two of them lunged for the intruders, while the third one ran to the oversized window and took flight.

The two remaining birdmen expanded their wings as they leapt for Alexandros and Ludlow, who were now entering the room. Red ran in after them and quickly scanned the room. He had hoped he would see Nonie sitting there waiting for him, and when he did not see her, his heart sank. Instantly, his thoughts turned to the task at hand. He quickly jumped onto the back of the birdman who, by now, was attacking Ludlow. Red grabbed the birdman under his mighty wings and snapped them backwards, breaking them. Screaming in pain, the birdman fell to his knees. Ludlow took the opportunity to cast a Wizard Web around the birdman so that he was held where he knelt. Alexandros had the second birdman also on his knees, in a Wizard Web.

"Where is she?" Ludlow demanded. When neither of the birdmen talked, Red walked up to the uninjured bird man.

"Tell me where Nonie is or die!" He wanted it to be the birdman's choice. Red knew if the birdman did not tell him where his love was immediately, then he was going to drop dead, and just like that, he did. Red turned his attention to the second birdman, still screaming in pain with broken wings. This time Red did not say a word. After seeing what had just happened, this birdman looked at Red and said, "She is behind King Edic." He turned his head to the side and looked at the wall that was covered in a large tapestry of King Edic, while sitting on a white stallion.

Red rushed over to the tapestry and pulled with all his might. Down it came, crashing to the floor. Behind the fallen tapestry was a secret room, that containing three large cages. One cage was empty, one held Nonie, and the last one held three other women, who all had similar facial features as Nonie. All of the women had their feet and hands shackled to the floor, with gags covering their mouths.

As the sound of the crashing tapestry hit the floor, the captive women all sat up and faced their rescuers, instinctively sliding away from the cage doors. Their eyes were now opened wide and filled with tears of gratitude.

Red ran straight toward Nonie's cage and said, "Open." As commanded, all the cages opened, as well as the shackles. Alexandros and Ludlow rushed to help the other women get to their feet, while Red tended to Nonie. He quickly removed the gag from her mouth and kissed her without hesitating. He was so happy to see that she was safe, that he almost didn't realize how tightly he was holding her. Nonie, equally relieved to see him, returned the embrace and asked, "How did you find me? I cannot believe it! I thought I would never see you again!" She then began kissing him again. Suddenly, Nonie remembered that she was in the same room as her sisters and no longer shackled. Separating from Red, she scrambled to her feet. She rushed over towards her sisters, as her sisters were rushing towards her.

Red smiled as he watched them unite. The three women cried more tears of joy as they reached out to hold their long lost sibling. As soon as they all were joined together in the embrace, each sister felt a jolt of energy pass through them. It was as if an unseen force had revitalized the women right where they stood. Sadly, while Nonie's sisters were captives, they had been held indoors without the benefits of the sun. They were very pale and their eyes had looked lifeless, but now that the sisters were in the embrace, the women were full of energy and life. Being together was the key to their existence.

Suddenly, from the doorway, an unwelcome voice broke the energized silence.

"Well, well, well, what do we have here?"

King Edic stood, blocking the doorway with more birdmen. From the window, another birdman flew in and landed in a fighter's stance.

Standing next to Edic, was a beautiful, younger woman, dressed in a golden gown that shimmered in the light.

Edic turned to the woman at his side and said, "Seize them all."

"Yes, Mighty One," she replied.

Chapter 18
Mirawa

Mirawa did as she was ordered. She seized the group of strangers, with one of her simple binding spells. Once cast, no one could escape or produce magic against her. Instantly, Red could feel an invisible force holding him still.

"Now then, I see that we have some unexpected visitors," Edic said, as he began walking around his captives, who were now invisibly bound together, in the center of the room. Edic continued circling the group studying each person. He stopped finally, standing in front of Alexandros.

"Hello, Uncle. It's been a long time," Edic said, his voice overflowing with hatred.

"Edic. Tell me, how is your father, the *real* King?" Alexandros asked, resentfully. He was well aware that Edic knew the dark truth behind his question.

"Ah, yes...Father. Let's just say, he will no longer be a thorn in my side, or anyone else's, for that matter. So, do tell me, Uncle, who released you?"

"Why does that concern you? What's done is done. You are King now, and I can do nothing about it, right?" Alexandros scornfully replied.

"So, should I assume that you know it was I who locked you away, in the Room of Need?" Edic asked, boastfully.

"Yes, Nephew, I knew it was you, the moment the door closed because at that moment, my heart broke into a thousand pieces. I spent years wishing it were not true. You almost killed me by putting me in there. I also know that it was you who killed both your father and your mother. So here is a question for you... Do you enjoy sitting proudly on a throne of death and lies?"

"Ah, well it is true that I locked you away, killed my parents, and made myself King, but I have not lied. Ask me anything, and I will tell you the truth. I do not hide what I am. I merely use what is at my disposal, to get what I want. Isn't that true, my dear?" Edic turned to the woman in the gold dress.

"Yes, Mighty One," she replied subserviently.

"Where are my manners? Uncle, this is my wife, Mirawa. We met after my father...uh... died. I was traveling back to Lanzeville, when I stopped in the quiet little town to water my horse and walk about the marketplace. That is when I saw this little flower in a secluded alleyway. She was using her magic on a boy, who was bullying her. I have to admit, her beauty attracted me at first. But, when I watched what she had done to the bully, I knew I had to have her. Naturally, from that day on, she has not left my side. Isn't that right, my precious?" Edic turned to his wife and watched, as she held a weak smile. It was clear that she was not happy thinking about how shallow Edic truly is.

"Alright, now, let's get back to business. Uncle, you have yet to tell me who released you. I want to...thank them, properly," Edic sneered.

Red had been listening to the exchange between Alexandros and Edic. He felt the tension, but tried to keep his expression firm because he knew that with one badly-timed glance, Edic would know that it was he, who released Alexandros.

Memories came to him in a flash. Quick segments, popped into his thoughts, a door opening, a large dog laying on the floor in the Room of Need, the image of Alexandros shape-shifting from a dog into a man.

Pushing the memories aside, he noticed Nonie and her three sisters looking at him. He now knew that it was not just Nonie who could read his thoughts. Lucky for Red, Edic had turned his back to him. He had started walking towards the birdman, who had been standing at the window and did not see the four women staring at him.

Quickly, they looked away from Red and drew their attention back to the real danger... Mirawa. Oddly, she was now looking straight at Red, after she had apparently witnessed the exchange of looks. Red suddenly felt sick, thinking that he had made things worse. Fortunately, Mirawa did not reveal to her husband what she had just witnessed.

Once Edic finished speaking quietly to the birdman, he turned back to his captives as the birdman took flight, out of the open window.

"Shall we continue this over some lunch? I was about to sit for a meal and I would love to continue this conversation in a more comfortable atmosphere. My dear, if you would escort our guests to the dining hall," Edic motioned with his hands to Mirawa, who was to now make the captives walk collectively to the dining hall.

If Mirawa had to concentrate on her magic to make the group of seven do as she wished, she did so without showing any strain or stress. She was indeed, skilled in her craft.

Red wondered if he would be able to set them all free somehow, without accidentally hurting anyone in his party. He had learned many years ago, to think before he spoke. More times than he would like to remember, Red had caused a negative affect when trying to simplify a situation. He thought back to once when he was younger, when he tried to please his father by shortening a hunting trip. Instead of hiding in a bush for hours waiting for a deer or wild boar, Red spoke, "come to me." Instantly, an entire heard of bison, deer, and antelope, charged the forest. As quickly as he could, Red had climbed a tree to escape being stomped to death. It was a lesson well-learned. Since that day, Red had learned patience, and he also had learned how to fish, instead.

Today, he would have to think carefully and consider his words before speaking, unless he was prepared to suffer the consequences. He noticed Nonie had reached over and took hold of his hand, giving it a squeeze. With her ability to read his mind, she must have been listening in on his thoughts. Red felt embarrassed to unwillingly share such an awkward memory. With her hand in his, Red decided that he did not want to risk getting Nonie hurt.

The captives made their way through the castle and finally reached the dining hall, where there were very few furnishings in the enormous room. The table, being the centerpiece that seated thirty-six guests, was enough to fill it. Every picture hanging was of Edic, in a variety of settings and in the corners of the room, there were busts or statues of Edic, in various poses.

Mirawa forced everyone into high back wooden chairs. Red felt like a puppet being pushed and pulled into movements that he could not control. By the expressions on his friends' faces, they all felt the same way with the exception of Ludlow, because his awkward snail body and shell would not fit in a chair. So, Mirawa used her magic to pull a chair out of the way for Ludlow, so that he could now occupy the open space at the table.

Naturally, Edic sat at the head of the table, enjoying Mirawa as she directed his unwilling guests. Directly to his right, sat Alexandros, Ludlow, and then Red. Nonie and her sisters sat on the opposite side.

There was an awkward silence, as the prisoners sat and waited for what Edic would do next. Red noticed that Mirawa did not sit at the table. Instead, she stood slightly behind Edic, to his left. Red realized then that Mirawa was just as much a prisoner as he was. She was not a true wife, nor his equal. Sadly, she was just a slave to Edic's demands. With that same realization, came the idea that he may have an ally.

Without warning, Edic suddenly clapped his hands together, twice, causing Red to jump in his seat. Red had assumed the clap was meant to get his attention. He then relaxed because he realized it was only a signal for the kitchen staff to bring in the meal. In they came, a dozen waiters, carrying trays of food. They placed them in a single line down the center of the table. Next, there came a line of waitresses, carrying empty plates. They set one before King Edic first, then his guests.

"Let us eat." Edic announced, waving a hand before him as if he had magically made all the food appear. His eyes gazed across the roasted pig, honey ham, garlic potatoes, steamed carrots & broccoli, fresh baked bread and rolls, and a bowl of various fruits. Edic started to eat the appetizing meal placed in front of him. After a couple mouthfuls, he noticed no one had moved. He looked up and shouted, "What's the matter with all of you, why aren't you eating!"

Ludlow quickly snapped back, "What makes you think we wish to break bread with you?"

Edic, trying to remain calm, answered. "So here I am offering you my hospitality and you throw it back at me?" They all watched in disgust, as pieces of food went flying out of his mouth.

Now Alexandros stepped in and addressed Edic. With utter hatred, staring eye to eye with him, he announced, "I for one, will not share a meal with you and pretend that we are having a joyful family reunion. If you wanted us dead, then you would have done that in the tower. So just say it now. Why did you bring us here Edic? I want the truth!"

Edic, still maintaining his composure, casually took his cloth napkin off the table and wiped his mouth. He then, slowly sat back in his chair and put his dirty feet up on the table, landing them right on his plate of food, cracking the plate in half all the while, sending dirt and food to splatter onto the table.

"Ok Uncle Al, I will tell you why I have brought you here." Edic, then shouted over his shoulder, "Umtar, bring him!"

Just then, a birdman entered the room, pulling thick, heavy chains over his shoulders. The chains were attached to an elderly man, wearing a filthy, tattered, brown robe. He was shackled by the ankles and wrist; his head bowed down in defeat and sorrow. Red noticed that Umtar was the same birdman who had flown out of the window after Edic had spoken to him, in the tower.

Immediately, Mirawa noticed who the man was, that was being dragged into the room. "Father!" she screamed in horror. Edic looked to his wife, who was now red-faced and full of anger.

"Yes, my precious, as I have always promised, your father is still alive. But he will not remain so much longer."

Mirawa looked completely defeated. Previously, Red was afraid of her, but now he felt sorry for her. This confirmed to him that Mirawa was forced to be Edic's bride. Now Red knew for sure, that Edic was controlling her. If she did not follow his every command, he would have revealed that he had her father and used that fact to blackmail her. Clearly, now was the time to do so.

"Mirawa, I want you to kill my uncle, right in front of me. I want to see him die painfully, just as I watched his brother. I brought your father here to remind you of what I am capable of doing, in case you should choose to disobey me," Edic boasted, as he stood up and walked over to Mirawa's father. From his tunic, Edic withdrew a dagger and held it to the old man's throat. Umtar held the chains tightly, making it impossible for the old man to move.

"Don't hurt him! I will do it. May the Spirits forgive me, I will do it," she said.

"That's my girl, go on then ....do it!" Edic ordered, as he pushed the blade closer to her father's neck, causing the old man to flinch.

Red watched in shock. Would Mirawa actually kill Alexandros? Just then, Red noticed the magical bond holding him had vanished. He no longer felt the pulling sensation that had been keeping him in his chair. Still he did not move. He did not want Edic to know that he was free. He did not think that Mirawa had accidentally lifted the spell. No, she was too good to forget that she had prisoners. This was definitely intentional.

Red had just barely finished his thought, when the room went powerfully bright. It was as if the sun itself, suddenly had found a new home and instead of its massive presence staying in the sky, it was content to shine with all its might, into the dining hall.

Although Red was now temporarily blinded and disoriented, he thought he heard Nonie speak.

"Give me your hand."

He reached across the table for her, toward where he thought she was sitting, but he could not find her hand. Before panic could rise in him, he felt someone grab his arm and then squeeze it. It was Nonie. *How did she do that? The last time I saw her, she was across the table, now she's sitting next to me.* Red tried to comprehend how quickly Nonie had responded. He had not even absorbed what was happening, and yet Nonie was on her feet and by his side.

"Run!" Nonie shouted.

I can't see, Red thought.

"Trust me!" she replied, trying to sound reassuring, but he could hear the urgency in her tone.

He forced his feet to move, to run for his life. Red could not see the ground beneath his feet, yet he ran as fast as his legs would carry him. He could not tell if he was running away from danger, or right into the arms of death.

Chapter 19
Mirawa's revenge

The ground beneath his feet had changed. His footsteps no longer echoed off the stone walls, and instead were now quiet and weightless. Red gave Nonie's hand a squeeze as he ran which made his hand the only part of him that felt safe. He could not see, but he could hear voices around him. He thought he recognized the voices.

Is that Meme? Red asked Nonie, in thought.

"Yes, we are back in the Giant world. That's why you can't see where you are yet. We're still passing through the clouds. Look straight ahead, you should be able to see them any second now."

Yes, I can see them now.

"Good, let's keep moving. We will be safe as soon as we get to Thug's house," Nonie replied.

Can you tell me what happened?

"When I felt the bond from Mirawa release us, I knew it was she who had done this and she knew that we could read minds so, she allowed us to temporarily access her thoughts. She spoke to me and my sisters, in our minds. She told us to be ready to run. Mirawa was going to open a portal and send us into it, and we would have to run through or else we could die. You see, there are many types of portals. All portals are temporary, but they vary with how long they exist. Some portals can handle large groups. Some portals can only transport one or two people. Mirawa told us to run, so I figured it was only a portal for one or two. So, if we had one of those portals meant for one or two, we would have to run or possibly die. If you had looked behind you, you would have seen my sisters running right behind us."

Where is Alexandros and Ludlow? Red asked, wondering if his friends died in the portal.

"We will know soon enough," she replied.

Red felt a mixture of emotions. For the time being, he and the girls were safe, and that was a relief. Sadly, he still did not know if his other friends were safe, as well.

As they approached Thug's rebuilt house, the giant was standing outside.

"Nonie!" yelled Thug, as he noticed the group running towards him. The only part of them that was visible was their tiny heads, bobbing in and out of the clouds.

"Hello Thug, I missed you!" Nonie yelled, as she ran up to Thug and hugged his large leg.
"Nonie gone."

"I know Thug, I am sorry. We would have been crushed if we stayed," Nonie tried to explain to Thug, but the look on his face revealed his confusion.

"Nonie gone," Thug said again. Nonie laughed and realized any attempt at explaining would still be too complicated.

"It's okay, I am back now, and I brought friends!" Nonie said, waving her hand toward her sisters who were now wide-eyed, frozen with fear. Nonie turned to them and said, "It's ok, he won't hurt you. He has been like a big brother to me."

Thug was so happy that he started to clap his oversized hands together making a sound so loud, that Red, Nonie, and her sisters had to cover their ears. Nonie stepped away from Thug, just in case he stomped his feet in excitement, too. Instinctively, Shedoe, Hyori and Haslena also took a few fearful steps backwards. They kept their distance until the clapping stopped.

"Thug, can we go inside and wait for our friends?" Nonie asked.

"Mom of Thug there," Thug replied pointing to his home.

Thug turned and led the way into the house. Just before they entered, Nonie spoke to her sisters.

"Please do not be afraid. I have lived here since the day our family was torn apart. They are gentle giants. They will not hurt anyone. Trust them as you would me."

"Nonie, we have seen and done a lot of questionable things in our time, but this is a first," Shedoe explained.

"We can talk about all that later, but for now, relax and let me show you where I have been all these years," Nonie told them, as she put her arm around Shedoe.

As Red walked inside, he remembered what it was like to enter this house for the first time. He could imagine the thoughts of the newest visitors. Haslena and Hyori had walked inside together, and Nonie and Shedoe were still holding each other, when a woman giant shouted.

"Nonie home!" Meme shouted with a smile, when she noticed who entered her home.

"Hi, Meme. Good to see you," Nonie replied.

Meme walked over to Nonie's broken habitat that sat on the floor. She picked it up and brought it closer to Nonie.

"Thank you, Meme," Nonie replied.

Red walked over to Nonie and Shedoe. He remembered the first time he had seen Nonie's house. It looked like a large birdcage hanging from a wall and now it looked like a pile of broken twigs. He also remembered seeing the furniture inside. It had the most beautiful furnishings he had ever seen, and he had learned that Nonie had created it all. He clearly remembered her saying, "I know what they want to be." He wondered if she could repair it back to its beautiful state again. Nonie glanced at Red, smiled, and went to work. Once again, she was listening to his thoughts.

Nonie turned her attention to fixing the habitat, which had been badly damaged by the falling boulders. He watched Nonie close her eyes as she pictured in her mind what her home had looked like once before. She reached out with her hands and touched the wood. Suddenly, there was a surge of power rushing through her fingertips, which caused Nonie to open her eyes and when she did, she noticed that her sisters had also placed their hands on the cage and were now assisting her in rebuilding the habitat. They did not know what it looked like and she knew that they did not need to know, as long as it was in Nonie's mind. Her sisters were simply amplifying her power. The broken fragments began to glow and attach to other cracked and broken shards. One by one, the twigs that formed the elaborate cage twisted and turned to create a stable cage wall. The furniture inside looked as if they were alive. The chairs now moved and "healed" themselves as if some unseen hands were doing all the work. Within minutes, the habitat was repaired back to its original state, except this time, it was stronger and better than it had been before.

"Wow, that was amazing," Nonie proudly said, smiling at her sisters. At that same moment, she was overcome with so much emotion and that she broke down and started to cry. Haslena grabbed Nonie and embraced her. Shedoe and Hyori joined in. It felt so good to have her sisters back in her life and Nonie knew right then that her life and her abilities would never be the same again. Being together with her sisters and using their combined energy, was both incredible, and overwhelming at the same time.

"Impressive," came a woman's voice, from the doorway.

Everyone in the room turned to see Mirawa standing there. As she glided across the room towards them, Red instinctively positioned himself to stand tall next to Nonie. He knew that he would protect Nonie in any way he could, even if it meant losing his own life to save hers. Nonie touched his forearm and smiled at his thought.

"She is not here to hurt me, it is ok," Nonie assured him. She is the one who helped us back at the castle. Nonie then said, "Let her explain. Maybe then, we can finally get some answers."

"Make yourselves comfortable and I will do just that." Mirawa waited to start until they had all taken a seat inside Nonie's habitat. Then she began.

"It all started on the day when King Edic first found me. I was on my way to the market with my father. When we stopped to buy some fruit, I noticed a kitten stumbling around, most likely starving, and I wanted to help it. While my father was busy checking apples for bruises, I followed the kitten, trying to catch him, but he was terrified and kept running away from me. Just when I thought I would catch him, he would

get a jolt of energy and run off. I kept following him,
but that last time, when I thought I was close enough to
finally catch him, a boy appeared out of nowhere and
cornered me. He demanded money. I told him I did not
have any and he became angry. He was about to attack
me. I was afraid, so, I unleashed a thread of my power
causing him to lift slightly off the ground. His arms and
legs stretched out, his eyes rolled into the back of his
head, and his hair stood on end. That's when Edic
noticed me. He watched, as the boy screamed in pain.
When I finally released the boy, he collapsed, falling to
the ground. When he was able to make it back to his
feet, he ran, and never looked back. That is when Edic
came over to me and told me that I should go with him.
I told him I wanted to get back to my father. He assured
me that he would send someone to tell my father where
I was. Edic told me that I had to leave the market
before the guards were called and they would lock me
away. I was just a young girl and I was afraid. So I left
with Edic and he revealed his true identity on the way
to the castle. For years, I questioned Edic, but he
always made excuses as to why we could not go see
him. Maybe because I was so young, I just accepted his
answers. Regrettably, I had not seen my father since
that day in the marketplace.

In the beginning, he was very charming and he
won my trust. I started to share with him, more of my
abilities. I guess I was showing off a little, mostly

because I was excited to have someone interested in me. It was wonderful to have someone appreciate what I could do. My father, on the other hand, had always told me that I should hide my abilities and, I have to admit, it was nice being able to use my gift openly.

One day, Edic came to me and asked for a favor. When he explained what he wanted me to do, I declined because I did not want to be involved in anything that would be against what I believed was right. He became very upset with me because that was the only time he had ever asked me for a favor. He threatened me by saying, that if I didn't do as I was told, that innocent people would have to suffer for my insubordination. Naturally, I did not want anyone to suffer, and in that very moment, I realized that, just like everyone else, even I, was merely a tool.

When I was of age, I was forced to wed Edic. He told me that as his wife I was to obey him without question. So I always did, but yet, I secretly intervened whenever I could. Like today, when I destroyed the door in the tower. Of course, Edic had no idea I had spoiled his plans. If he did, then I am sure that he would have tried to kill me.

Today, when I saw my father for the first time in years, I was in shock. I always thought he had forgotten about me and just moved away, like Edic told me. I had tried to locate him over the years by using my "second sight", but never did I think that Edic would *have been holding him captive. Maybe that is why I never found him. I never thought to look inside the castle. When I saw him today, looking frail and sickly as if he had not seen daylight in years, well, my anger and hatred for Edic took hold and I unleashed my wrath. I released all of you and that bright light you witnessed, was a flux of magic. I opened two portals, one sent you all here, and the second one that sent my father to a place where he would be safe. Then, I destroyed the man who had almost ruined my entire life.*

I am sorry for many things that I have done over the years. First, I want to apologize to Nonie, Shedoe, Hyori, and Haslena. I knew of your parent's demise. Although I did not kill them, I feel partly responsible for their deaths. I should have stopped Edic. You see, Edic had heard of the power your family possessed, from his Readers. They are a group of women who can "read" or sense great power, and when they had revealed this to Edic, he wanted it. They knew he was a very jealous man, and since he had no magical ability, he wanted to control anyone who did. On the day your parents were killed, Edic sent out a flock of his guards. The men with wings were supposed to capture your whole family and bring you all back to the castle. No one was to be hurt.

So when I heard him give the order, I used my ability of second sight to watch the mission unfold and

I watched sadly, as the flock attacked your family, wrongfully killing your parents. When they took Hyori, Shedoe, and Haslena, I made sure that Nonie was not amongst the captives. Luckily for her, she was a short distance away from the others, so I opened a portal that sent her to safety. The portal was instantaneous. To her it would have felt as if she had taken only three steps, when actually it was a great distance.

Ever since that day, when Thug found you, you had lived with the giants, and I kept hidden, your life force from Edic. He looked for you, for years. He ached for your power. You see, his plan was to use your combined power to amplify my abilities. While Edic knew I was powerful, he had no idea just how powerful I was already. He never knew I hid your existence from him, or he would have tried to kill me.

Thankfully, for me, the Readers were kind at heart. They had a fondness for me ever since the first day I was brought to the castle, or they would have revealed the extent of my strength to him from the beginning. Even worse, they would have revealed my occasional insubordination.

Over the years, I masked the strength of your sisters' abilities, but not yours, Nonie, I never hid your powers from you. I wanted you to develop your strengths and discover your weaknesses. You have done very well. I am proud of your progress and recently you have discovered even more abilities since you left the giant world. You have been able to read minds, manipulate objects, and most of all, you can now connect to your sisters' abilities. You four women, have a wondrous ability to connect to each other in ways that even I have never seen.

When the time was right, I had to direct you away from the giant world. It was I, who made the giant land shake, so that I could lead you towards Lanzeville, which as we know, is where your sisters have been for all these years.

I must confess, I brought you all together for my own selfish reasons. I wanted Edic to think that he finally had what he was always searching for. Then, I wanted to take it all away from him, just like he had done to me. I also had to make it right. I could no longer let evil sit on that throne." She paused, and added, "Now, you know the truth of it."

"I don't know what to say," Nonie added quietly.

"I do. You heard her. She let our parents die because she wouldn't stand up to Edic," Shedoe said, scornfully. Then she quickly closed the space between herself and Mirawa. With an opened hand, she slapped Mirawa across the face. The sound was like a sudden crack of thunder, and it made all who witnessed it, flinch at the sound.

"No Shedoe. We are more than that," Hyori reprimanded, as she stepped between Mirawa and her enraged sister.

Mirawa responded imperviously, "She is angry and is entitled to be so. I will allow her that one outburst. But if she or any of you try to touch me again, they will not live long enough to regret it,"

Where do we go from here? Red thought. He knew the women could hear him and was hoping that it might change the tension of the room. They all, now, faced Mirawa.

"I wanted to bring you all to a safe place so that I may explain, and now that I have, I need to get back. You are all welcome to return with me. From here on out, your lives are your own. I will no longer intervene," Mirawa informed them, as she started towards the oversized door.

What of Alexandros and Ludlow? What will I find if I return with you? Red thought.

"They are alive," Mirawa responded.

"You want to return to Lanzeville?" Nonie asked, looking into Red's eyes.

Yes, I need to make sure they are okay. And besides that, he promised to help me find my way home. How would I find my way without him? Red responded.

"Then I am going with you," Nonie said, as she took his hands into hers.

"We will all go," Hyori finally spoke up. "We have been separated for far too long, and need to have a proper reunion. We will stay together."

138

Collectively, they walked towards Mirawa as she opened a safe portal for the group to step through.

Chapter 20
Great reunions

Traveling through the portal again was not as shocking to Red, as was his first trip. He knew what to expect this time. Yet still, he felt a little uneasy since last time he had to run and this time he was walking instantly through time and space. As he stepped through the portal, he was thinking about Alexandros. Red wondered if he had planned on staying in Lanzeville and becoming the rightful king. Now that Edic was gone, Alexandros would be next in line for the throne.

Red knew his thoughts were not his own these days, and that others could listen in on him, but that did not prevent him from wondering what Mirawa might do next. She, too, had said she needed to return to Lanzeville, but she did not say what she was going to do once she returned. *Will there be a battle for the throne?* He wondered.

As the group stepped out of the portal, Red recognized the room to which they had returned to. It was the kitchen where Mouse worked.

"Where else would you expect to find the wizard?" Mirawa said, in jest.

What they found instead, was a vacant kitchen. The staff should have been busy preparing for the next meal, chopping vegetables, baking bread, and selecting prime cuts of beef. "Well, this is odd," Nonie said as she noticed no one was in the kitchen. Just then the door swung open, as Alexandros pranced through carrying a basket of food.

"See, what did I tell you?" Mirawa said as she raised a hand towards Alexandros, as if she had just announced his arrival. "Oh, there you are lad, you're safe! We searched the entire castle for you," Alexandros said, as he set the basket down on a table and hugged Red then Nonie. Alexandros then went to the basket of food, took a loaf of bread out of the basket and started eating it.

"We were sent through a portal by Mirawa, and have just returned, Nonie stated.

"Where is everyone?" Mirawa asked, referring to the kitchen help.

"I sent the castle staff to assemble a town meeting. I believe there are matters to discuss," Alexandros said between bites of bread. He offered the basket of food to his friends. Hyori grabbed an apple right away. Haslena was a little more hesitant, but her hunger took hold and she grabbed two apples and a loaf of wheat bread. Shedoe took the bread from Haslena and broke off a chunk and started eating, too. Nonie and Red both grabbed fruit from the basket. Mirawa ignored the food.

She walked to the kitchen window and looked at the town below.

The sun was setting quickly as everyone in the kitchen continued filling their bellies. "We should be on our way. There is much to do" Alexandros said. Mirawa stepped away from the window. She straightened her gown and ran her fingers through her hair. "So it begins," she said, mostly to herself.

Red hoped Alexandros had a plan, in case Mirawa was planning to fight for the throne. Red glimpsed at Mirawa. If she was able to read his thoughts, she still showed no sign. How would he help Alexandros fight a woman so powerful? Red was new to the world of wizards and beings of magic. He knew they were both magically capable of a duel, but who would win in a battle? He remembered Alexandros talking about how he had to work hard at wizardry and spells. Mirawa on the other hand, seemed capable of just about anything and made it look easy. He hoped that he would never have to find out.

They had left the kitchen, made their way through the castle and down towards town, when they saw Ludlow waiting with a group of townsmen. "Ah, Ludlow, my friend, what say you?" Alexandros asked.

"The town's people are ready for the news, Sir," Ludlow replied.

"Good work," Alexandros responded, as he spied the crowd of people standing around. To the right side of the road, was a make-shift platform. Today, this platform would act as the gateway to a new world for Lanzeville.

Mirawa led the group, as they walked to the front of the crowd. People stepped aside for their queen, making an open path. When they reached the platforms steps, Red watched as Alexandros placed his hands on Mirawa's shoulders, embraced her, and kissed her cheek.

Mirawa walked to the center of the platform. She raised her hand to silence the crowd. As she greeted her subjects, Red listened intently while she spoke of her husband's unfortunate death. Mirawa did not say that she had killed King Edic. Instead, that he had been killed during that same training exercise that also killed King Ovarb years ago. Due to the fatalities, she had promised that those training exercises were now terminated. There would also be a reduction of patrolling guards, and no more final judgment. As she spoke, the people cheered at the promises for a brighter future, a better future without Edic. The people would be able to enjoy their own lives and not live in fear, any longer. Word was already spreading of Edic's death. It seemed the entire town was now spilling into the streets.

Once Mirawa had concluded her plan for the future, and the cheers had died down, she exited the platform to join her new friends. Nonie seemed surprised that Alexandros had not stepped up to be the king. "You don't want to rule?" Nonie asked Alexandros.

"No, Lass. Mirawa is queen. It is her place. She is strong of will and stronger of heart. She will be a fair and just queen. I can settle my heart knowing my home is finally at peace."

"Thank you," Mirawa said. Then she kissed Alexandros on his cheek. "If you will excuse me, I have to speak to the guards. I must see where their loyalties lie." Mirawa was now solely responsible for Lanzeville and had to return to business. She hugged Nonie and her sister, and again, apologized for their captivity. They would be forever welcome into the castle as guest of the queen whenever they wished. There were no longer any hard feelings against Mirawa, as the women said their goodbyes. Alexandros and Mirawa took a moment to speak privately. When they finished, Mirawa went to Red.

"I would like to give you a gift, if you will accept it. I know good things are bound for you and Nonie, and I want to assist you in any way that I can. This gift is my, "thank you". If it were not for you, Alexandros would still be locked in the "Room of Need and Edic would still be king. " Mirawa reached into her pocket and withdrew what looked like a Tiger's Eye marble. As she placed it in his hand, she said to him, "Take this. You see the orange coloring surrounding the center of blackness? That is a suspended portal. It can be used only once, to bring you and whomever you wish, anywhere you desire. All you have to do is throw it to the ground and concentrate on where you want to go." She then kissed his forehead and walked toward her castle.

Red could hardly believe what he had just heard. With his eyes and mouth wide open, he looked to Nonie and Alexandros.

"What did you say to her?" Nonie asked Alexandros.

"A wizard does not reveal his secrets," Alexandros said, as he laughed.

Thinking about his future and his chance to go home, Red turned to Nonie, *I was wondering, if I use this special portal to go home, will you, and your sisters, return with me? We are always in need of new teachers. The elders are...well, they are old and could use some help,* Red thought, knowing she was listening. He did not want to think of his world without her in it. He wanted to be with her always. It felt like a lifetime until she responded. Tears started to fall from her eyes. For an instant, Red's heart sank, fearful of her reply. After a moment, she composed herself and replied. "The moment I met you, my life changed forever. We have developed a bond that can never be broken. Being with you has also brought me to my sisters. Now we are a family again. Nothing will ever separate any of us, ever again."

Red knew that when he spoke to Nonie in his mind, that her sisters could hear him too. They knew his invitation was heart-felt and he wanted them to come too, and not just to tag along with Nonie. Hyori stepped forward and spoke, "I am willing to explore new lands and see the world that we have been denied for so long."

Haslena spoke next, "I would like to remain together, although I am unsure about teaching to a village that I know nothing about." Red nodded his agreement.

Next was Shedoe, "I, too, want to stay together. I'm in."

Nonie spoke up again, "Wait, what about Alexandros?" She asked.

"Oh lass, I spent many years as a canine and I would like to stretch my legs a bit. I may take you up on the teaching position in time, but for now, I wish to travel."

He turned to Ludlow, "What say you, Ludlow?"

"Sir, it is time for me to go, too. I should be getting back to my wife and children," Ludlow said in a bittersweet tone. "I expect you to keep in touch, Sir, once you have found your way and settled down." Ludlow moved closer to his mentor and friend. "It has been an honor and a privilege, Sir," he said.

Alexandros bent slightly to embrace his life-long friend. "It is I, who has had the privilege to call you friend, dear Ludlow." Alexandros straightened up and wiping a tear from his eye, continued. "You have not seen the last of me, I promise you." Ludlow then said his goodbyes to everyone else. Suddenly, in the darkening sky, fireworks colored the night. The people that remained in the street applauded for the show, thinking it was part of the queen's announcement. As Ludlow's figure grew faint in the distance so did the fireworks.

Although he did not know when he would see his friend again, he knew in his heart, that he would. Red embraced Alexandros, *Can you tell him I wish him well, and I will never forget all he has done for me.* Nonie relayed the sentiments to Alexandros.

"I know lad, and I will never forget you either. You are like the son I never had. Be well, and take care." Alexandros took his leave in true wizard fashion. He shape-shifted into the form he was most comfortable with, an Irish wolfhound. He ran towards the forest, and in the distance, he stopped at the edge of the tree line, let out a howl, and then disappeared from sight.

Red turned to Nonie and her sisters, *Ready?* He took the marble that he was still holding and threw it to the ground, at his feet. Simultaneously, everyone grabbed hands as the portal burst open. It looked just as it had in the marble; the orange glow surrounding a black center. Red was hesitant at first, unsure of how the portal would be able to find the Bonk Bonk village. Yet he concentrated on his village, his hut, and his family fishing together. Most of all, he thought about his mother and how he wished she would be waiting for him when he returned. Just then, a figure appeared in front of the portal. Tears stung Red's eyes as he noticed his mother's spirit calling out to him.

"Come, my son. It is time to return. You have done well. I am eternally proud." Shelu then headed back into the portal, leading the way. Red looked to the four women at his side and nodded. As one, they all joined hands and stepped forward until the portal enveloped them.

Chapter 21
Great changes

Their journey through the portal was smooth until the end when the group stepped out. They all were suddenly "thrown" by an unseen force onto Bonk Bonk land. At the moment of impact, Red felt a little dazed and disoriented yet he still started looking around for his friends. Red noticed Haslena and Hyori making their way to their feet, each asking the other if they were okay. Red went to Nonie to see if she was okay. Hyori was the first to see that Shedoe was sprawled out on the ground.

"Nonie, help!" she yelled.

Nonie was closer and reached Shedoe first, just as she started to sit up, grabbing her head with a moan. "You struck your head. Here, let me help you." Nonie offered, as she noticed the blood trickling from the side of Shedoe's head. Nonie helped her sister stand up while Red took hold of Shedoe's other arm for support. He glanced down at the ground and saw a rock with fresh blood dribbling down it.

"What do you think happened?" Nonie asked Red. When he did not respond she shouted,

"Red, say something to me with your thoughts!"

Red did as he was asked. He thought about traveling through the portal and what might have caused them all to be thrown to the ground.

"I can't hear your thoughts! Nonie, clearly distressed, now questioned her sisters. "Can you hear him?"

It was odd the way all four women looked at him now. They were all concentrating so hard, that their faces looked contorted. He could not help it, he started to laugh.

"You should see the faces you are all making. It's so funny."

All four women stared at him with their mouths wide open. He did not realize he had spoken aloud. He started to laugh again, but this time, Nonie stood still. She stared at him.

She said, "Red, you spoke!"

When he realized what Nonie had just said, he too, froze. He was the one who made the funny face now.

"I spoke...I did it again! What's happening? Well, I mean, nothing is happening, and I am still speaking." Red was in disbelief that he was speaking and nothing bad was happening magically.

"I wonder if all our other powers are gone, too. Hyori, lay your hands on Shedoe to heal her," Haslena said, forcefully. Hyori did as she was asked. She put her hands on Shedoe's head and closed her eyes. Soon after,

Shedoe's cut had closed and the blood dried and flaked away.

"I am still able to heal," she said, in confirmation. The look of relief was now clearly on all their faces.

"Once we stepped out of the portal and onto the Bonk Bonk land, we felt that pulse of power that knocked us to the ground. I wonder if that pulse altered some of our abilities," Nonie said, as she tried to figure it all out.

"Anything is possible," Red said aloud. "Come on, let's go into the village and see if anything else has changed."

Together, as a family unit, they walked into the village. When they passed the first hut and noticed the entire village sitting in a semi-circle, with a fire blazing before them, the group stopped. Red's eyes scanned the villagers for his family. He noticed them sitting next to the elders in the front row. The only sound was the crackling of the fire. After a moment, Red stepped forward.

Suddenly, the entire village broke out into cheers. It was the most noise that he had ever heard them make. He almost felt out of place. He knew that the only words ever spoken were in the schoolhouse as a young child. To hear the entire village cheer was overwhelming. It made his ears ache. His eyes began to water as he was caught up in the moment. One of the elders, who sat closest to Red's father, stood and walked slowly over to

Red. Not knowing what was happening; Red was too scared to move. He watched the elder stand before him, and when the villagers stopped cheering, the elder spoke in a raspy voice.

"You have fulfilled your destiny. You have broken the Curse and ended our silence. We are most proud and grateful." The elder, who was much shorter than Red, asked him to kneel. The elder removed a beaded necklace from around his own neck. He paused for a moment before placing it on Red, "From this day forward, you are an honorary elder," and then he set the beads around Red's neck.

"How could I be an elder? I am not worthy. The elders have years of life. I am just a boy," Red asked.

"You left here a boy and have returned a man. You have earned the title and the right. You are an elder," he said.

Red turned to Nonie. She was still standing with her sisters a few feet back. He extended his hand, wanting her to join him. He introduced Nonie and her sisters to his father, and the entire village.

"It is time for a celebration. Now, let's feast," Red's father shouted with joy.

As was the custom of the Bonk Bonk tribe, the women worked at the preparations for the meal. The men removed a large boar from the fire pit and began slicing the meat. After the meal, some men and women began dancing, while the elders watched. Red noticed Hyori and Shedoe had joined in with the dancers. Haslena sat with a group of children, and was telling them the story of an evil king who ruled an oppressed land. Red smiled as he looked around at everyone having a grand time. It felt good to be home and it felt even better having Nonie at his side.

Late into the evening, when everyone had long since had their fill of food, and the dancers were just too tired to dance, Red asked his father how he knew they would be returning today. With the glow of the fire lighting up their faces, Red noticed his father was smiling. He could not remember the last time he saw his father smile.

"Red, your mother came to me last night, in a dream. She told me that you would be bringing a great gift, and with that gift, great changes."

Red then asked, "If I made this happen by just coming home, then I should have used my words to bring me home sooner." Red said lowering his head and feeling guilty that he had not thought about it before.

Red's father put his arm around Red's shoulders and said "For years, son, the Elders had tried a great many things to break the curse but, when you were born, the Elders started to have visions of our future. You see, they knew it would be the combined power of your new bride and her sisters that would save us. As soon as you all arrived, just as foretold, the earth pulsed violently. As you know, our words alone would have never broken the curse like that. So, you see, it was never a matter of when you came home, but who you came home *with* that broke our curse. And now, everything has happened, just the way it is supposed to be." he explained, beaming with pride.

"But, Father, you have made a mistake, she is not my bride. We are not married." Red said.

Smiling, Red's father looked at Nonie and then back at Red and continued, "My son, there has been no mistake. You know first-hand the power of your words and how they can change your life forever."

Red was confused at first, and was now just starting to understand. Suddenly, before he could make complete sense of what his father was trying to say, Nonie took hold of Red's hand, looked into his eyes, and then said,
"I do!"

Made in the USA
Columbia, SC
30 November 2017